The Grandfield Servants

Hats of Destiny

* * *

Olwyn Harris

Published by: Reading Stones Publishing
Helen Brown & Wendy Wood
Woodwendy1982.wixsite.com/readingstones
Cover Design: Olwyn Harris. Some of the cover elements were created using AI Technology. The image of the house, 'But-Har-Gra' was obtained from Wikipedia.org and used under the following licences. Permission is granted to copy, distribute and/or modify this document under the terms of the **GNU Free Documentation License**, Version 1.2 or any later version published by the Free Software Foundation; with no Invariant Sections, no Front-Cover Texts, and no Back-Cover Texts. A copy of the license is included in the section entitled *GNU Free Documentation License*. And was modified by Olwyn Harris.

For more copies contact the publisher at:
Glenburnie
212 Glenburnie Road
ROB ROY NSW 2360
Mobile: 0422 577 663
Email: Readingstonespublishing@gmail.com

Authors Note

When I was twelve my parents were gifted with a holiday at 'But-Har-Gra' in Sydney. Staying in such an imposing manor-house captured the imagination of this country girl. I was fascinated by the tiled mosaics on the verandah; the grand sweeping polished timber staircase; the thick, wide internal walls that naturally insulated the rooms, so they were cool in summer; the grass tennis courts and the majestic Camphor Laurel trees in the garden. I also remember being told the house had been seconded by the government during WWI and was converted to a war-hospital for injured soldiers, and it became an orphanage in the second world war. The stories of this series are set in a similar house with a similar history. They fulfil a childhood wondering of who might have inhabited such a place, and what might have become of the servants who worked there.

~ Olwyn

Dedication

For Rebekah... who understands the shape of me more than most.

Part 1

The Grandfield Mould

1909

"Yes Mrs Tunstall, you know this really is the first proper crop of mulberries in town. Our tree is always the first to fruit."

Mrs Tunstall's mouth was firm as she looked at the girl presiding over her street stand. The child only had fruit because her son Pauly kept the flying foxes away by netting the branches. He watered the trees and mulched the gardens from the straw from the stable... even beating birds away with a stick. It was ridiculous how Anna pretended that she made that abundance happen. Typical of a Whitaker to make them pay for what they made happen to start with.

"So fresh." Anna crinkled up her nose and breathed deeply. She squinted in the sunlight and adjusted the basket. She hoped the angle of the light shining on the trestle table would make the colour of the berries seem richer, brighter... rather than wilted and squishy in the sun.

"You know deary... you really should wear a sun bonnet. It would be such a shame to tan such a nice complexion. One day you will agree with me Miss Anna. Boys may not be interesting for you now... but one day, when you are older..."

Anna quickly pulled her hat out from under the table and plonked it on her head. She tried not to roll her eyes. Her mother said her tendency to do that was disagreeable and very unladylike. "You know, Mrs Tunstall, it would be such a treat for the men to have a special dessert to celebrate their win. Pauly says he does enjoy pie."

Mrs Tunstall tilted her parasol curiously and looked at this child presiding over her little street-stall as if it was a city avenue boutique. "Hmm."

She knew exactly what her men liked. Horses and football. In that order. Little else. Still, Ann had referred to her Pauly as a man. That was a recognition that most were unwilling to give. "I doubt he says that."

Anna quickly passed her a drink of lemon cordial, the cup sticky on the outside. "When I have my riding lessons Pauly tells me your pie is the best. Or... you could try a special crumble topping. Marlie's recipe is a favourite with all our visitors."

Before Anna could launch into another sales pitch, Mrs Tunstall put down the sticky cup without drinking it, resigned. "I suppose I will take two cups," she said impatiently. Even if Pauly wouldn't eat them, she did like fresh berries with custard.

Chrissy helped fold up the paper cones and put a cup of berries in each; Anna took the coins in her purple stained fingers and counted them into her pouch.

"I'm glad you decided to take them now, Mrs Tunstall. There won't be any left by the time the game is over. I am definitely sure I would not like Pauly to miss out," she said, as she officially entered the purchase in her little notebook and added up her running tally.

Mrs Tunstall shook her head again, balancing her purchases with a string bag over her arm and her parasol in hand, she walked up the driveway to the residence designated for the Grandfield Park stable manager.

Chrissy jabbed her. "Anna! You are telling a lie. Pauly Tunstall never says he likes fruit pie. Only meat pie."

"Humph. Fruit pie... meat pie... I didn't say which. Pie is pie. It is not like he doesn't enjoy pie at all. Besides, if they win the game, they will be happy to eat any pie. And if they do lose, they will be too devastated to care. Either way, it is close enough not to be a lie."

"Oh!" Chrissy's face blanched as a shadow passed over the table.

Anna jolted as she stared into the freckled face of Billy Stamford. "What do you want Billy?" she said, glaring sternly at his grubby fingers, poking at the basket of berries.

"Oh Anna, just let them be," urged Chrissy stepping right back.

"We're goin' to the footy game," he said. Billy's sidekicks smirked as they lined up along the table. One of them took a fist full of berries and gulped them greedily, purple juice dribbled down his elbow. "We need snacks."

"Well, the game is nearly over, so you'd better hurry."

"Nah, I reckon not," said Billy carelessly, giving a nod to his mates.

"This is a holdup," said one of his minions.

"Yeah!"

"Hand over your takings!" said another.

"Give it to us..."

They spoke all at once... a scrappy attempt to sound unified in their heist.

"No! Absolutely not! These are our earnings," Anna said determinedly, pushing her eleven-year-old pigtails out of the way, and clutching the bag to her chest as she stood her ground.

"Hogwash. You're a silver-spoon livin' on Parkland Avenue. You got enough and ya don't deserve nothing more."

"Anna... please. Just let them be..."

"No! We picked these berries ourselves. We've earnt every penny."

"If we say they's is ours there's nothing you can do about it."

"I'm not giving anything to you!"

"Don't have to, 'cause we're just going to take it," said Billy confidently.

"Then you're going to have to fight me for it. You wouldn't hit a girl!" she declared boldly.

"Wanna bet? I can hit a girl as hard as any bloke."

"You wouldn't dare!"

"You dare me?"

"Yes! I dare you!" said Anna burring up defiantly.

Billy leant over the table and slapped her hard across the face and then punched her in the belly, winding her hard. She gasped and doubled over! She could hear Chrissy screaming. The shock of his audacity took Anna's breath away; tears streamed down her face. It was not the stinging of the slap or being winded that hurt, but the lack of respect. The disregard of common courtesy left her face smarting with humiliation more than the strike itself. His knuckles connected on her lip, and she squealed with another wave of shock. She leant over gasping, and he reached forward jerking the bag from her fingers that refused to let go.

"Oi! You there! Get out of here!" Richard came tearing down the driveway. Billy's mates scattered like cockroaches. Anna went to chase them, but Billy turned around and shoved her to the ground before he took off down the road, waving the loot in his hand. "Hey? Are you okay?" Rick said crouching down, using his handkerchief to pad her lip.

He looked up at his sister trembling. "Oh Rick! She's hurt," cried Chrissy, compassion tearing at her little heart.

Anna paused. Her eyes stung and she stilled the quivering on her lip by pressing his kerchief firmly against it. Rick escorted her to the shade and then poured a drink of lemon cordial. She gulped it, inhaled deeply, and then wiping her mouth one more time, she stood tall. "I am okay. It didn't hurt that much. Except when he said we didn't do anything to earn this. But we did!

We worked really hard." She surveyed their stall, stained, and messed up. "Now the table does not look so good for after the game."

"They're bullies. Take no note," Rick said pouring refills of lemonade, and helping himself to some spilt berries.

Anna took the cup and sipped it slowly this time. The cut on her lip started to sting. "But they took our money!" That hurt even more.

"I know. So, will you let me stay now? Having another person around might help."

"You just want to eat our profits!" she declared, her blue-grey eyes flashing in defiance once more.

"No. I want to stay because you are two against a lot. Anything that hunts in packs like that, targets those away from the herd so they can take them down. If I am here, it makes for a bigger herd, tis' all."

"That's ridiculous. Chrissy is here with me."

"And yet your money pouch is missing," he said, his teenage eyes crinkled with his smirk.

"Why aren't you at the game? Even Mother went with Father."

"Cricket season is over... and I happen to prefer the strategy of chess to watching grown men fight over a pigskin like girls at a tea-party."

Chrissy gasped. "Rick! You can't say that. Daddy says that just because you fancy something different doesn't make it wrong for other people." She straightened the things on the trestle and covered a stain on the tablecloth by rearranging the basket. "Oh Anna. Just let him sit by and read his stupid book. He won't get in the way."

Anna looked at him with a tilt of her chin. "Just remember Rick Barnes, we don't need you interfering in our business. And you must swear an oath not to tell Mother!"

"Sure. I will just sit over here, but I will need a cup of berries to buy my silence..." Chrissy gave him a cup as he pulled a book from inside his shirt and settled down in the shade. "... and as I am not likely to encounter your mother, I'm pretty sure embarrassing yourself with 'common commerce' won't come up."

"Oh Anna! Your lip! What will you tell your mother?" Chrissy fiddled with the things on the table and arranged the cups over the stains on the cloth.

"Humph! She won't notice."

"Of course she will notice. It's on your face!"

Anna giggled. "Oh. Well. She might not notice. Tibby is going to let me know when he leaves to collect them, so we have time to pack up before they get home. I will wear gloves, so she won't see the stains on my fingers. And if she sees my lip, I will simply say I fell over. That is not a lie... even if it was at the hand of Billy the Bully." She straightened up and flicked her pigtails. "And, if I tell her I was practicing my deportment exercises and tripped on a stone, it will be less distressing for her."

Chrissy shook her head in admiration. "Oh Anna. You come up with the strangest excuses."

"It is not an excuse... it is an explanation." To prove her point, she went over and snatched Rick's book from his hand. He groaned his irritation and shook his head as he tried to retrieve his book.

"Anna!"

Anna skipped away and put the book on her hat, walking along a line in the pavement. "See, I can be a lady. In fact, I already am."

There was a deep cough, and someone cleared their throat. "Good afternoon ladies..."

"Oh, Reverend Peters!" A pang of guilt flashed over her face as she quickly let the book drop into her hands and she passed it back to Rick. Had the Reverend come to call her out on her fib about Pauly's affection for pie? Or fabricating the cause of the misfortune that befell her lip. Or both. She cleared her throat and gathered her manners. "Good afternoon, Reverend. The game is over already? What was the score?"

"10:4/9:6… in our favour. It has been a very exciting semi-final all the way! I couldn't stay any longer as I have an appointment I need to attend. No doubt you will have plenty of customers coming by soon."

"You look very warm. Would you like a drink of lemonade? It's complimentary. I made it from the lemons grown in our very own orchard. Perfectly refreshing."

Rick put his book on the table. It was a book about chess with a large Rook embossed on the cover. "She means my mother made it. As such, it comes highly recommended."

"Regardless of who owns the recipe, I added the water," said Anna determinedly.

"Well, if it is Marlie's lemonade how could I pass?"

"You can have the pick of these freshest mulberries before the rush. Does your wife enjoy berries-and-cream? Reverend, wouldn't that be a lovely treat? She works so hard work for all our parishioners."

"You make a heart-warming case Miss Anna. I will take four."

"Four! Oh. That is generous. Let me put them in a bag for you." She riffled in a box under the table and pulled out a used paper bag.

"I do hope you will continue coming to our Community Choir Anna. Miss Lambert is very pleased you are joining our little group," he said pulling his coins out of his pocket and putting them on the table.

Anna forced a smile. "I like singing," she said politely. The choir was not as fun as she thought it might be, and her mother said it was 'amateurish and crude'. She believed a private Repetiteur was more in keeping with how a daughter of Grandfield should be taught music. The fact that the same singing teacher worked in both places had no bearing on that preference.

The Reverend nodded and grinned. "Well, thank you for the berries. I trust you will not be engaging in commerce on the Sabbath tomorrow."

"Oh Reverend, the berries are far too delicious to expect there would be any left over. Your concern about me breaking God's law is needless." At least she meant the law about keeping the Sabbath. She was a little bit uncertain about bearing false witness. Perhaps she needed to work on that.

The Reverend looked at his watch and then he paused, eyeing the cut on Anna's lip. "I saw the Stamford boy with a couple of his mates running from this direction. It seems like they were up to no good."

Anna turned her head away and demurely covered her mouth. "I couldn't say Reverend," she murmured. She wasn't going to be caught tittle-tattling. That was a sin her mother insisted was a larger crime than breaking the sabbath or any white lie. "They said they were late for the game."

Chrissy mutely ducked her head when he glanced at her.

Rick retrieved his book from the table. "I think it was timely that you happened by Reverend," he said. "These berries just get snatched up by all sorts coming by. They have made quite a bit of money."

"Well, Mr Barnes, I take your point. Take care of your charges," he said, tipping his brimmed hat. He had notice there were no other coins in her little coin bag.

Anna watched him adjust his dog-collar, and hurry onto his appointment. "Rick Barns," she said primly. "I will remind you that *your* parents work for *my* parents. You are not in charge of me."

"I am well aware, Miss Anna," he said, as he went back to his possie by the tree and opened his book unperturbed. He glanced up to see Anna glaring at him fiercely. "What?" he asked with a raised brow.

"Richard Barnes! Don't forget your station," she said emphatically.

"That will not be likely. You remind me often enough."

She quickly changed her frown to a smile as she saw a stream of fans coming up the road, decked with red or blue scarves and talk of the game. Anna celebrated their victory or shared the indignation of having their win snatched away right at the end of the game. Many cups of berries were sold. Rick helped Chrissy keep up with the demand by filling paper cones with a scoop of berries in each and standing them in drinking glasses on the table, lined up for a quick sale.

Anna was helping Chrissy serve out the last berries from a box under the table, and Rick had retreated again to his book under the tree, when a customer cleared his throat. "Ahem. Are there any left?"

Anna quickly stood up, swept her braids back and flushed prettily. "Oh Constable Trey! Good afternoon. Yes, you are in luck, we do have a couple of cones left. A few coins are a small price for a healthy body and alert mind."

The Constable nodded seriously with a twinkle in his eye. "I do need to be alert in a job like mine." He dug deep into his pockets for some loose coins. He noticed the cut on her lip and the tear in her stocking. "I am following an anonymous report of some untoward dealings in this quarter.

Assault, burglary, theft. You have a good view of the street. Did you hear or see anything?"

Anna's eyes grew large and instinctively covered the cut on her lip. Then she shrugged, looked up and down the street, and shook her head. "We have been busy with our stall."

"This is not the first time that reports of this nature come my way, and the culprits are not yet apprehended."

Chrissy looked away. Rick closed his book and stood up. "Do you enjoy chess, Constable Trey?" he asked indicating his book. "Sometimes I think our community is like a chessboard. The bishop piece would be like Reverend Peters. He passed by here earlier. Perhaps you would be the knight – upholding the law..."

"Hmm?" he said dubiously.

"One strategy I have seen recently, is how the knight is placed directly between the opponent's pieces and the queen." He stepped in front of Anna. Constable Trey looked at him with a frown. "But a pawn that is close by can lie in wait for an entire play, ready to make their move until the Knight moves away... and then comes in to steal the game." Rick took a step to the side, tilted his head and stared across the street.

Constable Trey looked at him keenly. "I see what you mean," he said seriously. "Well... in the interests of protecting Queen Anna and her King... one defeat on the football field is enough for today." The Constable put down his berries on the table and turned on his heel.

Anna stammered after him as he walked across the avenue, reached into the shrubbery, and grabbed Billy's collar. He lifted him out of the garden bed and placed him on the path. His mates scattered like marbles. While Billy was spluttering his innocence Constable Trey made him turn out his pockets. The money pouch, a few bottle caps and his lucky-tor marble spilt on the pavement. Trey guided the agitated Billy back to the stall, to return the pouch and its contents, with promises not to press charges if restitution was complete. Anna counted its contents and compared it to her ledger, nodding her agreement that all was square. Billy glared vengefully, and the Constable reminded him that he was fortunate an anonymous tip had exposed his very poor choice of hideout because now he was no longer a fugitive from the law. Trey sent Billy on his way with a clout under his ear and a warning under his belt. He tipped the short peak of his uniform hat, picked up his cones of berries, nodded his farewell to the street venders as he left. Anna watched him walk up the street with a bewildered frown.

Tibby pulled the phaeton out of the driveway and gave Anna a wave with his driving gloves as he passed. "Just going to collect your parents Miss. They will be finishing their after-game drinks, so I'll be back in about half an hour."

She nodded, waved back... and quickly started to pack up the stall. She was removing the tablecloth when she stopped and turned to Rick with narrowed eyes. "Rick Barnes, did that talk with Constable Trey have anything to do with chess?"

Rick just shrugged. "No. Nothing at all."

"How long were they over there?"

"They slid in there when you had that rush of customers. I suspect they were waiting for the tally to go up before they swooped in for their final instalment. See I was right. Safety in numbers."

* * *

2.

"Now Annabelle, be sure to put on your new dress, and I have instructed Hillman to braid your hair. I need to talk to Marlie about the hors d'oeuvres, so don't be tardy." Evaline Whitaker turned on her heel, paused and turned back to her daughter. "I need you spotless to welcome the young ladies who are our guests. Annabelle, look sharp. We only have a short time to be ready, so don't be slovenly."

"Mother, the party is not until this afternoon."

"Annabelle, how many times have I reminded you that a well-prepared hostess is a well-regarded hostess. Now off you go."

Anna dragged her feet and pulled herself up the stairway. She knew which dress would be laid out on her bed, which hat, which shoes. She sighed. She had wanted to practice tennis this afternoon. None of the young ladies coming considered tennis a suitable activity for a Grandfield High Tea. She wandered over to the window looking out over the trees from her second story lookout. She saw Rick climbing one of his favourite camphor laurel trees. Anna flew down the stairs past Hillman in her apron and cap. "Miss Anna! Your mother wants me to braid your hair!" Hillman called after her. "Come back!"

"Back in a tick! Won't be long."

"Miss Anna!" Hillman rolled her eyes and wondered how she would navigate her employer's disfavour if Miss Anna went missing again.

Anna flew around the back, and then paused, before she sedately wandered over to the large spreading tree where Rick was reading his book in it branches. "Rick!" she said, surprised.

"Oh, hi Anna. I thought you would be in a flurry of preparations for this afternoon," he said, looking down at her from his perch.

Anna deftly climbed the branches and sat beside him. "Oh, it doesn't take that much to get ready. Why aren't you helping?"

"Because I do what my mother asks of me... and I do not play truant," he said pointedly. "I know Hillman is looking for you, so don't disturb me. I'm studying."

"What are you studying for?" she said matter-of-factly, looking over his shoulder.

His frown melted into a grin, and he went back to his book. "What do you think I am studying for? An exam, you duffer."

"What exam?"

"Hmm. Languages this week. English and Latin." He shook his head and turned a page.

"Huh." She sat for a bit but was quickly bored. She could not understand how Rick loved his books so well. Her tutor, Mr Meade made Latin verbs a laborious exercise in endurance. "Well, I am not skipping out. I will be ready when I need to be. I wanted to check that Chrissy will be coming to our afternoon tea today."

Rick tilted his chin and looked up from his book. "Anna, you know that is not possible."

"Why not? She is my best friend."

"Because she is helping our mother... with *your* mother's preparations. I believe they are up to their elbows in petit fours at the moment."

"It's not fair that she can't come!"

"Then you need to talk to your mother about who is invited. Not me."

"But she never listens!"

He grinned.

"What's so funny?"

"Perhaps that is a family trait Anna. I sympathise, but I can do nothing to solve this for you."

"Huh! You are so annoying! Today is going to be terrible. No one who is coming even likes me. It is not fair!"

He shrugged, but when she didn't move, he sighed and closed his book. He stuffed it in his satchel and buckled the strap. "I know. Look, I am going to my tutoring now, but you are catching up with Chrissy tomorrow." He leant over in a conspiring whisper. "And it is her birthday, remember. So why don't you have your own afternoon tea in the backyard after we get back from church? It's our day off, and I'll stand look-out... while I study. That way you won't be interrupted, and you can have all the fun then, that you can't have today."

She tilted her chin and then smiled. "I think I like that better. Let's do that. Will Marlie save us some things to eat?"

He nodded and hitched his satchel over his shoulder, swung down from the branches and landed on his feet. "I have to go now, but I'll mention it to her."

Anna watched him go. Rick might be Chrissy's big brother, but by default, he was her brother too. Better perhaps. He wasn't nasty like the brothers of the other girls she knew. Her own brother, Maxwell, was fourteen years her senior, and she hardly ever saw him. It was good when he was home, but that only really happened at Christmas time. This was her special secret, and it was a secret that she would never tell. Adopting the Help as your family, when you are a Whitaker... that was not good form. But Anna didn't care. She shrugged, swung down from the branches of the tree, and then turned on her heel and went along the wide, sweeping verandah, stepping and skipping across the patterned mosaics on the floor like hopscotch.

"Hey Tibby," she said, dodging the chairs he was carrying outside, to place under the marquee.

"Miss Anna... is everything ready for your guests?"

"Nearly," she said with a grin. Nothing looked like she was ready at all. "I saw Rick – he's on his way to tutoring now; Chrissy is helping Marlie in the kitchen; and you are setting out the chairs. I would say everything is on track."

Tibby laughed indulgently. Miss Anna was a twenty-five-year-old woman in an eleven-year-old body. "It seems you have your finger on the pulse. You make a lovely hostess Miss Anna." He moved and Anna followed closely behind him. "It is okay Miss Anna. I can do this while you finish what you need to do. That is what being a team is, isn't it? Each one doing their part."

"But this is more interesting than having my hair braided. Hillman is so rough. I wish Marlie could do it."

"I'm sure Marlie would love to do it... but if you give Miss Hillman plenty of time, so she is not rushed, and you explain what you need, even having your hair braided may be more tolerable."

"Please let me help you instead. I want to."

"Perhaps, but what would your mother say if your pretty party dress had smears on it?"

"This? Oh. This old thing is not my party dress."

Tibby laughed. "Well, it takes a true lady to make a play dress look like a party dress. Go and change... and let Miss Hillman braid your hair in the offending style, then you can come and supervise setting the table. And I promise not to tell," he added in a conspiring whisper with a wink.

Anna nodded and took off. She took particular care with her dress. She really wanted Tibby to notice the difference. She chose matching ribbons and pretty clips and didn't complain when Hillman tugged her hair too tight and pinned her hat so firmly.

When she returned, Tibby looked up from placing the silver on the pressed linen tablecloths and gasped with amazement. "Oh Miss Anna! Now I see what you mean. That is a very pretty party dress. And your hat matches your outfit so perfectly." Anna could hardly figure why that was noteworthy. Her hats always matched. "Did Miss Hillman do your hair? It looks so charming. The perfect hostess. What a nice way to package up a kind heart and kind words. Here. Did you still want to help? I have the serviettes in these baskets. You can place them around, just one at each setting. We will be very particular to put them here, just so... like this. Then, if you would like to arrange these vases in the centre of the tables, that would be very helpful." They went to work amiably chatting over silverware and crystal.

Quite suddenly, Tibby came over and took the basket from Anna's hand. She looked up, to object, but he winked and smiled. "Yes Miss Anna. I see what you mean," he said stepping back. "I'm sure your mother will agree."

"Tiberius! Isn't this finished yet? Where are the centre vases?"

"Ma'am? Miss Annabelle was observing that if the arrangements are put out too early, they would start to wilt. Having fresh centrepieces is a priority for a Grandfield Spring event. Limp stems look so very disheartening." He respectfully adjusted a limp stem as a point of emphasis.

"Humph! Of course. Make sure to spray them with the atomiser. Annabelle? Why are you not getting ready?"

"I am ready Mother. Hillman has braided my hair."

"Oh." She stopped and focused on her daughter's outfit. It was faultless. But she adjusted Anna's hat anyway. "Well don't get in Tiberius' way. He doesn't need distractions while he is on a timeline."

"Thank you, Ma'am. Miss Annabelle has a very keen eye. She has been checking the floral arrangements. I think they are improved by her critique. I will place them shortly."

"Of course she has an eye. She is a Whitaker." And she abruptly turned on her heel and left.

Anna visibly relaxed and giggled, scandalised. "Oh Tibby... you almost told a lie!" It was fun that finally she was not the only one be accused of this crime.

"Not really, because when you finish placing the linen, you will help me correct and place the centrepieces." He winked again. "Unless you skip off on me, and then I could legitimately be accused of being less than honest."

"Oh no Tibby. That would never do. Now I am obliged to help you with the flower vases."

He nodded with an affectionate grin. What a gem. His Chrissy would never use words like *obliged.* "Ahh, Miss Anna, you are a character, no doubt. Let's make these centrepieces the prettiest spring posies that Grandfield has ever seen. Should not be too difficult... since you are an expert on pretty."

Anna hummed and fussed and arranged roses and assorted spring flowers their **Chinese** gardener had picked from the garden. Finally, they stood back and admired their work together. "What do you think Miss Anna?

Is this a satisfactory setting for hosting a spectacular seasonal High Tea? Will your friends be pleased?"

"I doubt it. Nothing pleases them. They are all so snobby and rude. I prefer not to call them friends."

"Well Miss Anna, you cannot make them behave. Perhaps they are 'Tea-party buddies' instead of friends."

Anna frowned. "Still sounds far too familiar."

"Well Miss Anna, your responsibly is merely not to be snobby and rude with them. God has given you a wonderful nature, so do everything you can to protect it. When it is your turn to manage Grandfield Park, you will be kindest, most gracious hostess ever to hold an afternoon tea, regardless of the season."

* * *

"Marlie, why didn't you go to church this morning? Are you quite well?" Anna frowned when she discovered this extraordinary deviation from their weekly routine.

"I am very well Honey. The Lord and I had a special time together at home. It was Chrissy who was not feeling well, so I let her sleep."

"Oh no! Does this mean we will not be able to have our tea party this afternoon? I have it all set out."

"She was a little weary from all the goings on yesterday, 'tis all. It was a big day, but she did marvellously well. But I wouldn't entertain postponing your afternoon tea. No, not at all."

"Thank you Marlie. But you mustn't tell Chrissy," said Anna in a conspiring whisper. "This is the best surprise ever! I took the handcart with all our things, down to the bottom of the garden. I have our picnic all set out in the 'Secret Glen'. Are you sure she will come?"

"Oh Honey... you are the sweetest friend. Now here is the basket I put together so two little princesses can have their own special birthday afternoon tea in the garden. "Well, I am going to get Chrissy up now. So how about you check all is ready at your end? Tibbs and I will bring her down when she is dressed."

"Oh!" Anna turned away and gasped in dismay, her eyes wide. She had forgotten to get Chrissy a gift!

"When you are ready Rick will carry the basket down for you," said Marlie with an affectionate nod. "Hang it in the tree until Chrissy gets there, so the ants don't beat you to your feast. We will be down there about half two, so plan on that and don't get impatient."

"Yes Marlie," she said as she quickly ran to the nursery and accosted Hillman with the terrible omission of forgetting a gift

"Anna you are giving her a party in the garden. That is its own gift."

"Yes but, mostly I was just mad because we couldn't spend time together yesterday. Oh dear. What am I going to do?"

"You will think of something. What about ribbons? You have so many."

Anna tilted her head. "Do you think my blue dress will suit Chrissy's complexion? I could choose a different one for her to wear."

Hillman shook her head. "The blue is Chrissy's favourite on you, so I think she will be pleased with your choice."

"Or perhaps I should choose another? Should I wear blue as well?"

"You will look pretty with whatever you choose." After Hillman helped her change, Anna grabbed her bag of ribbons and tucked a small box in her hand and charged down the stairs to the servant's quarters.

Rick was standing there with his ever-present leather satchel of study books over his shoulder and the picnic basket. "Come on Anna... are you ready?" he said as he opened the backdoor to the kitchen. She followed him out into the garden, past Marlie's herbs where the gardener was turning the soil in a section of the vegetable patch. Anna knew the old gardener was Hillman's father, but she still thought it was strange to spend time with a gardener every day.

Rick walked with Anna through the grounds, climbed over the bottom fence towards Anna's Secret Glen. "What's in the box?" he asked suspiciously looking at the small box in her hand.

"A gift for Chrissy. It's not much, but I have to give her something."

When they arrived at the alcove, Anna looked around with a contented sigh. She always thought it was wonderful that Chrissy had her birthday in Spring when the weather was divine, and the garden was splashed with colourful, sweet-scented flowers. This glen was a beautiful little alcove, down in the far bottom corner of the property, hidden away, under the spread of large liquid amber trees. They had shifted a couple of garden benches to nestle in this pocket of garden, so it could be enjoyed in every season. Even late in the season it was still sprinkled with climbing roses, jonquils, miniature violas, and those cheeky little jolly-jump-ups, that spread their happy faces and gorgeous fragrances unbidden and unwitnessed most of the time. Then in Autumn, the plants snuggled under the rich blanket of royal coloured autumn leaves.

Rick put down the basket on one of the bench-seats and pulled the handcart over to the little garden table setting. Anna pulled out a white cloth and placed a china teapot spilling over with one of the flower arrangements from yesterday in the centre of the table. She arranged two settings of fine china teacups, saucers and side plates, crystal glasses, silver cutlery, and stiff linen serviettes, tied with pink satin bows.

"Show me what is in the box," said Rick with a determined set to his mouth, as Anna placed it beside Chrissy's serviette.

"No. It is for Chrissy. Besides, you will think I am stingy and mean."

"Noo... I think you might be giving something away that you are not supposed to."

"Humph. Very well." She opened the box to reveal a little glass bowl. When she lifted the lid, inside were two matching hairpins with a simple flower button threaded on each. "Crystal for Chrystal. I have a pair of these bowls, so now we have one each to put our hair pins in. And Chrissy is having a garden birthday party, so flowers are appropriate."

"Oh. That is actually nice."

"Don't sound so surprised. I can be nice."

He grinned at her. "I said that the bowl with the hairpins was nice."

"Pfft. I know what you meant. You think I am spoilt and snobby and rude. Well, I am not. I am going to be a nurse when I grow up."

He laughed. "You. A nurse. Don't be ridiculous Anna."

"I can be caring and kind." She really wanted him to see that she was different to the other girls who had turned up yesterday.

"Of course you are. Look at what you have done for Chrissy. You don't have to be a nurse to be kind."

Anna tilted her chin. "You don't think I can do it. But I can. I want to do something important... something different from Grandfield... something different from yesterday."

"That is a worthy ambition. But nursing?" He grinned again. "I can't see it. And besides, your parents would never agree."

"Humph. Well, what are you going to do? What is all your book study for?"

"Maybe a manager of a business somewhere. I have to the end of the year to finalise my choices."

"Well, I think you are brave to choose something different from what your parents do. I want to be brave too. I am going break out of Grandfield... regardless of what Mother says."

"Ah yes... your mother is quite emphatic about Grandfield standards," he said with a chuckle.

Anna tilted her head and flicked her hair. "*Oh Annabelle, what you are wearing is not appropriate for a daughter of Grandfield*," she said, mimicking her mother's lilt. "A house cannot be my mother, and if I want to be a nurse, I will!" she said emphatically.

He laughed again. "Good luck defying her wishes,"

"I have thought about it, and nursing is the bestest, most selfless, most worthy profession."

"I cannot disagree. If you say you want to... I guess you will. You tend to get your own way Anna Whitaker."

"Well, I'm glad you realise. Now Marlie said we had to hang the basket, to avoid the ants. And I thought we might decorate Chrissy's chair... her birthday chair, in flowers, and blossoms, and ribbons, while we wait." She picked up a cloth bag full of ribbons and pushed the hand-trolly back into its hiding place in the bushes.

"Are these your hair ribbons? That's a lot."

She laughed. "Some of them. And yet I still cannot always get them to match!" She rummaged through the bag and pulled out two blue ribbons and an assortment of other spring-coloured ribbons that she carefully matched with the flowers in the teapot. "You wrap the box in these ribbons since I didn't wrap it properly. I will start decorating her chair with these."

He shook his head and rolled his eyes. "Yes Ma'am."

"The blue ribbon's matches Chrissy's dress very suitably," she said. "Sometimes Hillman does have a good idea."

"Chrissy only has the dress on loan for your afternoon tea. She won't need the ribbons to match, you know."

"Of course, the dress is not a gift. Marlie would never allow it. But I have nearly outgrown it... and Hillman did say it was Chrissy's favourite."

"You are giving away your dress? What did your mother say?"

"I would not know, because I didn't ask her. I will say sorry and plead for another. Mother will understand."

"She will? Are you sure about that?"

"Of course, especially when it will probably get a tear or a stain... something like that."

"Unbelievable."

"Quickly – wrap up the box in the ribbons. I will start the chair." She busily twirled the ribbon around the back of the wrought iron lacework. She adjusted the cushions. And then she produced a pair of scissors and gathered some flowers and blossoms from the garden, poking them in amongst the ribbons and ironwork. She stood back, thoughtfully considering her creation, and then added some greenery. "We can set out the food now. She will be here soon."

Rick pulled down the basket and Anna arranged the tiered china cake stand with petit fours and savoury hors d'oeuvres that had been boxed up from yesterday's leftovers. Then she put two little cup-cakes in extra tea-cups added for effect, one with a taper candle poking from the top. Anna looked at it and paused. "Hmm... I think it needs something." She went and gathered a couple of tiny violets and arranged them around the base of the candle. "There. That is better. Shh... I think they are coming. Let's hide."

"You want to hide? You stood up to Billy the bully, yet you want to hide from your best friend? Stand your ground Anna Whitaker and be the courageous hostess that you are."

"But I want it to be a surprise," she whispered.

"It is already a surprise. You watch her face as she comes around the corner. You won't want to miss that."

They heard Tibby, Marlie and Chrissy talking as they strolled along. "They are taking a long time to get here..." whispered Anna.

"Shh. Don't be impatient... they are coming. Remember... watch her expression."

They could hear her admiring the garden as they came closer. "I wonder if the jonquils and jolly-jump-ups are still out. They were all in bloom for my birthday last year. This is the prettiest corner of the garden."

"It is very special," said Marlie sagely. "Just like you."

"Oh!" Chrissy stopped suddenly. She stood mesmerised by the tea setting before her. Her eyes were wide, and her lips parted, dumbfounded.

Anna ran over to her, clapping. "Surprise! Happy Birthday Chrissy! We are going to have our own birthday tea party. Especially for you! Since you didn't get to come to the one yesterday."

Chrissy hugged her, dancing. "Oh Anna! This is so beautiful. I feel like a princess," she said twirling in Anna's blue church dress that she had borrowed.

"The dress is yours. It is too short for me now."

Tibby and Marlie stood watching with a smile. "Well ladies, we will not interrupt you any further. Enjoy your own special high tea."

"Oh no," exclaimed Chrissy. "You must stay and share our afternoon tea with us. Surely there is enough for everyone!"

"Oh. I suppose it would feel like it is an important afternoon tea if there are more guests," said Anna dubiously.

Marlie quickly looked over at Anna, who was staring at the setting with a frown. "Miss Anna? Are you sure?"

"But I... I only set the table for two. I could go and get more settings from the kitchen perhaps."

Tibby stepped forward. "Now Miss Anna, let's think about how a true hostess would quickly make two settings go around five. You have glasses and cups... sufficient for the drinks. You have saucers and side plates... Marlie and I can share. There is no need for you to go back to the house and interrupt your time together."

"But Tibby, I wanted it to be perfect. I really did."

"And is it perfect. I know it can be disappointing when the picture in our head is different to what it looks like on the table. But do you think it is the setting and the china... or being with friends, that makes for the perfect celebration?"

Anna sighed. "Of course. Well Rick can move those garden benches to each side of the table. He can have one side, and you and Marlie can have the other. She quickly split up the settings, placed the birthday cupcakes on Chrissy's plate, and rearranged the table so everyone had a plate, a glass, or a teacup to sip lemonade with the elegance of fine dining.

As Chrissy took her place in the decorated seat of honour, everyone held hands as Tibby said grace. "Dear Father God, thank you for our special family, and precious friends. Give a special blessing to our Birthday Girl as we share this birthday feast. Amen."

They sang happy birthday. Anna presented her gift. Then she pinned ribbons in Chrissy's wispy hair with the pins, creating a soft colourful tiara with spring flowers, adding rosebuds and soft leaves for effect. Rick shrugged and stated he didn't know where the chair ended, and Chrissy began. The perfect camouflage!

"Oooh! Now you look like a princess. Princess Chrystal!" gushed Anna.

"I feel like a princess!" giggled Chrissy.

Rick laughed. "That would made Dad, King Tiberius, and Mum, elegant Queen Marlie. And I would be a prince – since Princess Chrissy is my sister. The only one here without a title, might be Anna,"

"Nonsense! Don't you know I am the visiting regent from the neighbouring realm. Princess Annabelle bestowing my presence on my best friend for her royal birthday. I am honoured to meet you, your Royal Highness... Your Majesty..." she said, bowing to Tibby and Marlie, who waved royally, playing the game. Anna and Chrissy made crowns of flowers and leaves suitable for a king and a queen. They raised their teacups, topped up with lemon cordial in a regal toast and ate their afternoon tea most delicately. They laughed uninhibited, enjoying the mystery of being happily transported to another place, and another time, with love and imagination.

* * *

3.

"Psst Anna!" Chrissy pulled Anna's hand and tugged her in behind the hedge. "I am glad I found you... because you must have dinner with us tonight."

"How can I have dinner with you? Mother will not let me skip out on a weeknight. I am not allowed to visit for dinner unless it's Sunday when Hillman is off. It's not Sunday."

"Ma said your parents have a thing that they have to go to. Mim won't tell."

"Mim?"

"Miss Hillman... her name is Mim. You know that."

"Oh. It's the social games night again... already. Then... perhaps..."

"You know, don't you, that Aunt Phoebe is coming? I will not survive without you being there."

"I have met your Aunt Phoebe before. She is not... interesting."

"Exactly. That is why I need you there."

"But Chrissy... she is so peculiar. I don't want to have to explain my hats... again. Perhaps you could come over to my room instead, and we could share sandwiches together in the nursery. Let's have a picnic on my bed." Eating on her bed was a most rebellious gesture. That would be an adventure.

"Pa would not let me. You know I must attend to our family dinners, especially when we have visitors. And we're not having sandwiches. Ma is making her special meatloaf..."

That Anna would consider eating dinner alone in the nursery with Hillman in preference to Marlie's special meatloaf, was saying something regarding her reservations about Aunt Phoebe.

"Oh Anna. Please..."

"Well..."

"And Ma has made those lemon tartlets that you like. There are lots of lemons at the moment. Please..."

"Lemon tartlets. With meringue? Hmm. Very well. I will just have to make sure I wear my best hat," she said with a sigh.

* * *

Anna bobbed a curtsy. "Good evening, Ma'am." She eyed the collection of hat boxes near the hall stand, and the large, brimmed monstrosity on Aunt Phoebe's head, overflowing with faux flowers and ostrich feathers.

"Child, I must say your hats have improved since I last visited. A well-fitting hat makes all the difference to any person... whatever the occasion." Aunt Phoebe's personal proverb was frequently recited.

"Then we should have a delightful evening together," said Anna with a curtsy, hiding her smirk.

Aunt Phoebe frowned as she stared at the brim of Anna's hat as she bobbed. "Humph. Notice how your hat slips when you move? It is a little sloppy." Actually, she meant it was *very* sloppy!

"My mother paid a lot of money for this hat. She said it was in keeping with our Grandfield style."

"No doubt she did. But money does not always buy the best craftmanship. There are milliners and milliners... if you know what I mean."

Anna nodded soberly; and had no idea what she meant. She removed her hat and hung it on the stand.

Aunt Phoebe's took it down and examined in inside of the band closely, reading the label of the maker with a frown. "Humph! I'm not surprised. Overpriced while the sewing around the band looks like a rat ran around there. Unbelievable!" She fretfully considered it a great wrong to pay significantly for something so poorly made. "I think these feathers are a little pretentious for one so young... even though you have always been a precocious little thing," she said as she returned it disgustedly to the stand. She removed her own hat and put it on the hallstand with a flourish.

"Now Phoebe," said Tibby guiding his sister-in-law to the table. "It is time for dinner. Plenty of time to talk hats later. Come. Marlie's special meatloaf is awaiting our attention."

They sat and said grace.

"Young Chrissy!"

Chrissy jolted in shock. "Yes, Aunt Phoebe," she quavered. Chrissy squirmed anticipating being subjected to intense scrutiny on some matter. Even meatloaf did not seem enough incentive for this.

"All young women need to be well versed in a practical education. I have a place for a young apprentice at the Millinery. I have been speaking to your mother about it. My shop is more like a studio than a store... a place for creating fabulous art, not just fashion."

"Oh..." Chrissy didn't find the fabulous art of millinery at all interesting. Her eyebrows shot up in fear as she wondered how she would survive the inevitable analysis of her life goals, and her wardrobe and a placement among hats all day that she didn't want to be part of.

Anna looked at Chrissy, and then at her meatloaf. She quickly cleared her throat with a corresponding twinkle in her eye. "Aunt Phoebe... are you sure it is okay that I call you Aunt Phoebe, Ma'am?" she asked innocently. "Us not being family and all."

"Well, it would be ridiculous if you didn't Child. You have known me since you were a baby, just as much as young Chrissy here. Don't start putting on airs now you are getting older. Of course you must call me Aunt Phoebe."

"Well thank you... Aunt Phoebe. That is very amiable." Anna studied her meatloaf again composing her thoughts. She chewed slowly and swallowed, before she looked up. "Aunt Phoebe, could I ask you a question? I do apologise Tibby. It is a hat related question."

"Of course." Aunt Phoebe looked at her expectantly. Tibby squinted curiously and took a sip of tea. Marlie quickly got up to bring the gravy-boat to the table, that had been left on the bench.

"I wanted to ask... how do you make so many excellent hats with just one block-head."

Tibby's eyebrows shot up high; Chrissy kicked Anna under the table; Anna choked on her meatloaf and spluttered ungainly. Rick smirked around his mouthful of meatloaf and quickly grabbed the gravy-boat when Marlie sat it on the table. He focused hard on lavishing gravy over his meatloaf and vegetables. Anna quickly took a sip of drink and innocently looked with wide eyes at Aunt Phoebe, the quality maker of fine hats.

If Aunt Phoebe noticed any of these strange contortions, she gave no indication. "No milliner of note would have only one block! First and foremost, it is essential to acquire a diverse selection of solid milliner blocks. If you don't have a quality block, you are not going to be able to craft a quality hat. I have a whole wall of wooden millinery blocks, and even some porcelain ones. I have just about every size and shape and style available. I call my shelves of milliner's blocks, "My Hatters' Library". And it is a matter of pride that I have used every single one of those blockheads. I will not acquire a block that I will not use. How many people do you know who have large libraries full of books, but never actually read them? A block is selected at the start to form and shape and mould my beautiful creations. Some people think that hats just appear in hat boxes on top of their wardrobe, but it is a matter of pride, of course, that I educate on the skill and effort that goes into each and every hat. Perhaps Child, you should come and visit my studio-shop, so I can show you what it takes to make an excellent hat. It is a craft... that it is..." and the white noise of her explanation continued... joining the buzz of crickets outside the window. Fortunately for Anna, Aunt Phoebe didn't need a response, she just needed permission to talk about her obsession. Anna watched Chrissy's shoulders relax and she was now enjoying her meatloaf. Anna went back to eating her own meal, and she smiled and nodded randomly, and didn't listen to anything that was said.

"Anna? Anna!"

"Oh. Yes Marlie?"

"Can you please help Chrissy clear the plates while I serve dessert?"

Anna nodded and quickly stood up and gathered the dirty plates. She enjoyed being part of this family. It never occurred to her that Marlie should ever treat her differently from her own daughter.

After dinner, Rick escorted Anna back through the main house to the nursery. As they were walking up the stairs, he stopped and cleared his throat. "Anna?"

"What?"

"You look so innocent... but at dinner, I thought you were being pert and insolent."

"That's ridiculous. Aunt Phoebe wanted to talk about her blessed hats. I just gave her permission."

"See. You think that because you have a pretty smile you will get away being cheeky with the adults. But it wouldn't be a bad thing to show more respect."

"It is only a problem if the person takes offense. Aunt Phoebe did not look the slightest bit offended, except when she realised my mother had paid her hatter too much for shoddy workmanship. I was doing her a favour... and I saved Chrissy from being enlisted into a millinery school when all she wants to do is cooking like Marlie. If Aunt Phoebe had to talk about something, it was better that she was talking about her stupid blockheads."

He shook his head as he continued to climb the stairs. Anna scoffed and put on an Aunt Phoebe voice. "Don't start putting on airs with me now Richard Barnes. I saw you. You were just as amused as I was at the start. It is ridiculous that you are pretending to be all high and mighty about it now."

"I am not pretending."

"It really would not surprise me if Aunt Phoebe had a block called The Grandfield Mould. Those hats would fit you perfectly." She was annoyed that he refused to appreciate her intent to protect Chrissy. "You are more Grandfield than I am."

"Perhaps you should worry more about choosing your own hats and not mine."

"I know my taste in hats quite adequately. You should show more gratitude and appreciate a well-made hat!"

"It is because I know you, that this is exactly my point." Rick opened the door to the nursery and handed her over into the custody of Hillman. "Goodnight, Anna of Grandfield, wearer of grand hats." He bowed and shook his head with a smile and left Anna with a frown on her face.

***

4

"Ahem, Miss Annabelle, what a splendid hat you have!" The deep voice of a gentleman, spoke so fine and properly, that it made Anna turn around with a gasp as she looked into the face of a young man dressed in a suit with tails. Suddenly she melted and ran to him in a rush and gave him a hug. "Max – you are here! Don't you look all dandy in your hat and tails!"

He lifted her high with a flourish. "Well Miss Annabelle, we are Whitakers. Dandy hats are a requirement. You have yours and I have mine."

"About time you came Max. Christmas is almost over. Why are you so late? Mother has been checking the driveway on an hourly basis for days."

"Late? Tomorrow is the fourth of December... the first Saturday of the festive month. I hardly call that the conclusion of Christmas."

"Yes, but Mother has been getting all the Christmas stuff out. And you know once she starts, it has to happen instantly. It is like the whole world stops until it is done... and it always has to be done before you get home."

"Well, I am home now, for the Gala as usual. I am glad my arrival means everything has been accomplished in a timely manner... as it should." He looked her up and down with affection. "But it doesn't seem like you have stopped growing despite the seasonal agenda. Look at you, Little Sister... you are becoming so tall."

"Mother says it is my deportment lessons. Marlie gives credit to her good cooking. Mr Tunstall says it is my riding lessons. Mr Meade, my tutor, says my fluency in Latin makes me grown-up. All of which is ridiculous... except perhaps the food. Why does everyone want to take credit for the natural process of growing?"

Max laughed. "Why indeed? Or... it could be all just the illusion created by a well-placed hat and no one should get the credit at all. Tomorrow night is the Christmas Gala, so I am trying on my suit. I would not want to embarrass myself at this illustrious annual event. Does it meet your approval?"

"Sure... if you tie your bowtie properly."

He adjusted it promptly. "Is that better?"

She shrugged. "Well, at least they let you out in public, because I will be hidden away with Hillman in the nursery. I cannot attend until I am sixteen."

"Hillman?"

"My governess...". She pointed to Hillman across the room, who was deep in a discussion with Tibbs, about using left over Christmas ornaments for the Nursery.

Max looked at her curiously with a frown on his face, and I thoughtful glint in his eye. "That is your governess? Huh. Does she read you 'The Three Billy Goat's Gruff'? She looks like she could do a grumpy troll-voice well enough."

"No. No one can do the voices of those Billy Goats like you. All that 'trip-trip-tripping' over the bridge is never the same. She makes me read it myself because she says I complain that she doesn't do it right. I am pretty sure you are responsible for all my nightmares about bad, angry trolls."

"Grrrr! I will always be your Troll, Little Gruffling."

Anna laughed. "And I will always be your sweet-talking Gruffling."

"I won't be able to call you my little Billy-Goat-Gruffling much longer. You will soon be too big for such stories. Perhaps you already are."

Anna shook her head and giggled. Her brother might be the absent member of her family, but he was also her hero, riding in at just the right moment to save her day. It was wonderful when he was home, because he didn't always toe the Grandfield line. Or if he did, he managed to do it with enough brazen cheekiness to make it acceptable. Everyone loved Max, staff included. The best thing about Christmas was having her two most favourite people at home together, Max and Chrissy. Max piggy-backed her back to the nursery, conspiring together how to get through the Gala and the other Christmas occasions on the calendar with the most amount of fun. Max always made things exciting. But what was least fun, was when he went away again, straight after Christmas.

* * *

5.

"No! No-no-no-nooo! Marlie! Marlie!" Anna burst through the door. "Marlie! Tell me that Hillman is lying. Tell me Chrissy is not badly sick!"

"Shhh, my Sweet. Shh. It is true. Chrissy does have a fever. We called for the doctor and... and we are trying everything to see that she will recover soon."

Anna stared at Chrissy's flushed face on the pillow. Her hair was wet with sweat, and the sheets stained dark from the water that Marlie used to persistently sponging her skin. Chrissy's eyes were half closed, glazed in delirium. She was murmuring incoherently about fire, and hot coals, and dinner burning. Chrissy coughed, and Marlie wiped away the phlegm streaked with blood that she spluttered up.

Marlie wrung out the cloth and gently wiped her daughter's brow again.

Anna tugged it out of her hand. "Here. Let me do this. Oh Marlie! She is terrible sick. When is the doctor coming?"

"He has already been and will come again... later this evening."

"Oh Marlie. I am so scared. What can I do?"

"Shh. Anna. Your Mother is calling. You go. I know that you care." She gently took the cloth from Anna's hand.

Anna scrubbed her eyes and reported to her mother. She was instructed to go to choir practice at the community hall. Anna had wanted to go to choir. She had begged her mother to allow her to sing in the choir. But not today. Today she needed to stay home and be with Chrissy.

How Anna got through choir was uncertain. And for the first time in her life, Tibby was not there to pick her up. Anna tilted her chin, adjusted her hat and walked home by herself. She went straight into Marlie. Chrissy seemed worse.

"Where's Tibby? I thought he would be here, since he didn't pick me up. He should be here... praying. He does that! He should be here!" Anna cried.

"I know my Sweet. He wants to be... but there were things that your mother required."

"How could you let him go? I will tell Mother that it is a terrible thing that she would not let him stay. He must come back!"

"Shh... Anna, darling. He will be back soon, and he can do nothing more here than what we are already doing, and he can keep the peace out there. I told him that he can pray anywhere. It is true. He doesn't need to be here to petition God for his mercy on Chrissy's behalf."

"Can't we do something more? Anything?" Anna's hand trembled as she wiped the cloth across Chrissy's brow. "Oh Marlie. She is positively burning up!" Her throat restricted tightly in panic. The night of the Gala seemed forever ago, Max had organised for Chrissy to come and have picnic under the Christmas tree with her in the nursery. The girls had laid under the Christmas tree all night and laughed so hard at their unfunny jokes about their Chrissy-picnic, and Chrissy-presents, and Chrissy-holidays, and Chrissy-hats!

Now Max had gone back to his Max-life; New Year's had been celebrated with the required number of parties; Rick had recommended his classes at school and Mr Meade was again haunting the Nursery with his frown and his lesson books and looking at Hillman with his very weird uncomfortable glances. Every routine had resumed like it did every New Year. Except this time Chrissy was sick.

Marlie came and took the cloth from her trembling fingers. "Anna darling... you should go. You shouldn't be here. Not in a sick room. Your mother would never allow it."

She stood up tall and straightened her back. "If I am going to be a nurse, then being in a sick room is something I have to get used to."

"Perhaps Anna... but not today. Not with Chrissy, whom you love like a sister. You need to let me look after her today."

"No. You cannot expect me to go. I want to stay. I need to stay. Oh Marlie, please. Please don't do to me, what Mother did to Tibby. Please allow me the kindness of being here. When she is better, I need to be able to tell her that I stayed through it all."

"Chrissy knows that you love her. As do I. We would never question that."

"But *I* will question it if I don't stay. I *must* stay!"

Marlie looked at her and swallowed. Her eyes were exhausted, glazed with the anxiety of a frantic mother, trying to keep it together. "Very well. We nurse her together. If the truth be told, it does me good to have you here."

"Okay good. What can I do?" She looked about the room, and then her gaze rested on the cloudy water in the washbowl on the stand beside the bed. She quickly stood up, and left to change it for clear, clean water. Then she went and made Marlie a cup of tea. The benefits of all those years of pretend tea-parties now became real. The tension in Marlie's face relaxed as she sipped her drink. "Thank you, Anna. You have such a kind heart. You will make a beautiful nurse if that is what you choose."

"What do we do for Chrissy now? How do I help nurse her?"

"We keep doing what we are doing. The doctor said we just have to wait for the fever to break. So that is what we do. We keep sponging her face and arms. There is nothing else."

"Nothing?"

"No, there is nothing but waiting and praying. But..."

"But what?"

"Well. There is something... I need to get a message to Rick. I wondered if you could give Pauly this note and ask him to go and deliver it to him. Rick is at school. I have written down the address, and this letter explains why I require him to come home."

"Marlie, you can't send Pauly on an errand like that. He is... the stableboy." Inflexible. Incapable of thinking outside the usual. Anna's tea party buddies called Pauly *that idiot tack-boy*. But he could look after horses. That he could do... obsessively.

"Well, there is no one else here who can go. Please. Just ask. There is a chance he would do it."

Anna stood up and nodded resolutely. For Chrissy and for Marlie. She could walk home from choir practice by herself, so she could deliver a note. If climbing high mountains would prove Chrissy meant the world to her, she would climb this mountain. "Marlie, I will go to the stable and make sure Rick gets your message." Anna picked up the envelope and tucked it in her pocket.

Marlie had already turned back to the bed and was murmuring as she wiped Chrissy's face. "Thank you. I am relieved. Rick needs to be here."

* * *

Anna made a decoy mess and when she was sure Hillman was busy cleaning it up, she grabbed her riding habit and crept over to the stables. She found Pauly muttering in the tack room, rubbing down the saddles. "Hi Pauly," said Anna brightly.

Pauly was tall and always looked the Granville part, in his smart stable uniform. But Anna didn't like him. Not really. Whenever people commented on his particularly chiselled chin and the handsome colour of his hair, all Anna could think was that it was a shame that someone good looking, could be so, so, *so not* fun. He had very strict rules about how to look after horses, which he would never compromise. He would fly into a temper if any of his rules were broken. Given that flexing rules was something Anna had a particular propensity for, Pauly got angry with her often. Anna learnt Pauly was best to be avoided. Tibby would tell her to be patient with Pauly, and to notice all the things that he could do well. And it was established that he was very good at handling the horses. But Anna also knew what he could *not* do. Taking the horses outside the designated exercise times, broke Pauly's rules. And unless you were Mr Whitaker. Or Tibby. Or Mr Tunstall – Pauly's father, rules could not be negotiated. Mr Tunstall looked after the stables and reinforced the rigidity of these rules on a daily basis.

Pauly looked up from his rubbing and nodded. "Hello Miss Anna." He went back to his saddle.

Anna wondered how to proceed. "Pauly, are you forgetting something?"

"No Miss Anna. Mr Tibbs has taken Mr and Mrs Whitaker out in the Phaeton. I am rubbing the tack today. Today is Wednesday."

"Wednesday is my new riding day. I am here to go riding." Anna thought that rather than breaking an established rule, making a new one might give her some margin.

He looked up and a furrow creased his handsome brow. Suddenly his face broke into a grin. "Oh Miss Anna. I get it. You are messing with me. Wednesday is Tack Day. Not riding day."

Anna spoke firmly. "Well sure... Tack Day. But now it is both Tack Day and a riding day. Didn't your father tell you? I have been doing so well at my lessons that I now go riding on Wednesdays as well as on Saturdays. See... I have on my riding habit."

"Pa did not tell me. I cannot do it unless he tells me, even if you wear your best riding clothes."

"But Pauly, I need a morning ride. If I wait until Mr Tibbs brings the Phaeton back for you confirm it with my Father, the time will be gone, and I will miss out. You know your father is the best riding instructor. How will I tell him that I have not been practicing riding like he expects? Mr Tunstall will not be happy."

"My Pa has gone to the saddler. He will be back soon. Why would he ask you to practice when he is not here?"

"Because he does the instructing, and I have to practice what he shows me. I do the same with my music lessons. I practice what Miss Lambert teaches me in my lessons during the week. I bet you hear me play my violin or sing when Miss Lambert is not here."

"Yes." He could not deny that what she said was true. "Your violin sounds like a cat stuck in a fence."

"Oh. Well, you see how important it is to practice... to get better. Your Pa tells me I am getting better at riding. But did you know, Pauly, that I think it is because the horses are so well looked after that I am doing so well. You are very good at getting them ready for me."

"You thinks I am good at getting the horses ready?"

"Yes. Yes, I do. Tibby has told me so many times as well."

"Mr Tibbs is very kind to me. Are you messing with me Miss Anna?"

"Pauly! I would never! It is important that I go riding today." With a little more cajoling, Anna's horse was saddled, he helped her mount up, and when he opened the gate to the exercise yard beside the stable, Anna turned the horse around and spurred him quickly out along the driveway and through the main gate onto the street. She quickly glanced back over her shoulder and saw Pauly, staring at her in horror, agitated by her blatant betrayal. Her stomach flipped. She reassured herself that she had not exactly told an out and out lie. Besides, her loyalty to Chrissy was the greater need.

The horse jogged down the street where Rick would disappear on his way to school. She reined up beside a cabbie and showed him the address. He pointed her in the general direction and told her the name of the street to turn down.

Anna pulled up outside the large stone gates. The arched sign indicated it was the right place. She frowned as she considered the address on the note Marlie had written. The avenue of trees lining the driveway, sweeping around towards the broad stone façade, with a columned portico and wide elegant steps looked like this was a place of serious scholarship. She had not expected Rick would go to a proper school. He was, after all, just the steward's son. But she tethered her horse on the street and jumped down, straightening her habit. She braced herself and marched resolutely along the driveway, her boots crunching loudly on the crushed gravel. She walked up the stairs and pushed open the heavy double doors. Every footfall echoed loudly in the empty corridor as she made her way towards the sign that pointed to the reception offices.

She wished that she had not worn her riding habit but had opted for a prettier dress. But the riding habit was needed as part of her ruse. She had to admit, getting past Pauly before he got angry was an accomplishment she felt quite victorious about. But she could not pause to enjoy feeling smug about this conquest just now. It was too important that Rick be told about Chrissy.

"Miss? Can I help you?"

"Yes Sir. I need to get a message to Rick... Richard Barnes. It is very important."

"And you are...?"

"Oh umm..." Chrissy was loved as much as a sister. Yes. She cleared her throat. "Rick... Richard is... ahh... he is my brother. Yes. I am his sister."

"Master Barnes is in his lessons. You will have to come back after classes conclude."

"But I have a letter from his... our mother. I must deliver it to him... in person. Now."

The man frowned and adjusted his double-breasted suit jacket. "You can pass the letter to me; I will see it delivered."

"No. I must do it in person." She tilted her chin and raised her brow as she clutched the envelope tighter to her chest. "I have been given charge over this message, and I need to deliver it myself. Tell me where his class is, and I will go myself."

"Miss Barnes? You do understand this is a Private Boy's School. A girl cannot be wandering about the halls like a stray cat."

"Our sister is very sick! I need to deliver this message." Her voice was strained, and her eyes burned with worry. "Would you have me talk to my parents?" This was a caution that usually caused oceans to part like Moses at the Red Sea. But it seemed that this only worked when she was the daughter of a Whitaker, and not masquerading as the daughter of house-staff.

He looked at her soberly and shook his head. He knew the Barnes family were of humble station. The enrolment had gone though many rounds of controversial discussion among the staff. If the student had not been so scholarly and a sporting asset to the school teams, or his enrolment sponsored – at least in part by the Whitakers, it would not have progressed. "Now I am positively terrified," he said blandly. He pointed to a bench. "Wait here, and I will have the scholar withdrawn from his class."

She returned the envelope to her pocket, sat down and looked around. There was a cabinet full of trophies. She stood up and went over to study its contents. She searched for familiar names among the shields and the prize cups and recognised some of the names that filled her parents' social circle. She spotted Rick's name on the debating team shield. There was a large cricket trophy made from the stumps and ball of some celebrated game. On the wall beside the cabinet there was a series of framed photos of each year the boys in their whites were holding that trophy with serious frowns. Rick was in a couple of photos, sporting his striped blazer and baggie school cap with the school shield embroidered on the front. He was tall compared to his team-mates and he stood in the back row. Anna was not surprised. She could not imagine any place where Rick would look out of place.

"Miss? I asked you to stay seated. Come this way please." He ushered her into a small waiting room.

"When is Rick coming?"

"Master Barnes is on his way. He seemed a little confused as to why his sister would be here if she was indeed sick. But he will clarify this situation shortly." And he closed the door behind him.

When the door opened again, Rick stood there in his school blazer and boater, with the student-master frowning beside him. Rick looked at Anna curiously with his brow raised and tried hard not to smile. "Young man... is this your sister?"

He cleared his throat, as he watched her wriggle on the spot. "Sir... I can assure you I have grown up with this person, and she irritates me as much as you would expect of any sister."

"Well then, I will leave you to your family business." He abruptly turned and left the room.

Rick watched him leave and then turned to Anna half amused, half bewildered. "What are you doing here Anna?" he said in a low whisper.

"Rick! I have a letter from your..." She stopped and cleared her throat; she spoke to the closed door very clearly. "The letter is from *our* mother. It is about Chrissy."

"Chrissy? What's this got to do with Chrissy?"

"Rick, she is sick. So very sick! She's got worse. Marlie wants you to come home urgently. She really did write you a letter." She delved into the pocket of her riding jacket and pulled out the crushed paper envelope and shoved it into his hand.

Rick suddenly was aware of her attire. "Anna, how exactly did you get here?"

"Tibby has taken my parents out in the Phaeton. Otherwise, he would have come himself. Mr Tunstall was out as well... um... doing something with saddles. Marlie wanted me to have Pauly bring you this message, but he just wouldn't understand how important it is, so I brought it myself. I had to do something."

"You rode! Here? By yourself? Does Ma know that? Where's the horse?"

She shrugged and tugged at his sleeve. "I tied him out on the street. You have to come now."

He scanned the letter, his frown knitting tighter as he read. He smoothed out the ceases of the paper and left it on the occasional table. He grabbed her hand. "Come this way…" He looked out the door and pulled her in behind him as they scampered down the corridor and slipped out a side door. They ran past the shrubbery, dodging behind a row of hedges to avoid the line of sight of the groundsman and gardener. A couple of sulkies drove in through the gates. Elegant passengers in large hats were enjoying the aspect of the imposing buildings before them. They crouched down and made a run for the gate to where the horse was tethered. Rick loosened the reins from a ring mortared into the stone wall. He hoisted Anna up into the side saddle and jumped up behind her. He leant over, grabbed the reins, and turned the horse for Parkland Avenue.

They cantered along the main road, overtaking all sorts of wagons, sulkies, and buggies on the way. As they were drawing alongside a particularly fashionable Phaeton, Anna realised Tibby was the driver, her parents were deep in some serious discussion. She held onto her hat, ducked her head, but couldn't resist a wave as Rick careered past. Tibby's eyes flew wide open, and his mouth dropped in shock. He quickly gathered himself and calmly pointed to the house on the opposite side of the road, attempting to distract his passengers.

But Mrs Whitaker was not to be distracted. "Riffraff," she muttered "Reckless youth! Don't they know the meaning of courtesy on main thoroughfares. And in his school uniform! Truant! That young man is bringing disrepute to respectable establishments. I should report him!"

Rick rode the horse through the gate and went straight around to the stables. He jumped off and lifted Anna down. He threw the reins to Pauly and nodded to him. "Good job, mate! You did really well Pauly," he called, and Pauly stood there stammering, staring at the horse's lathered withers as they both ran around to the servant's entry.

They burst into Chrissy's room. Reverend Peters was sitting quietly in the corner. Chrissy was still coughing and muttering deliriously. "Ma. We came straight away."

"Oh Rick, you are here! I was not sure Pauly would make such a trip. I have been praying and praying he would know what to do. It is so good you came my son," she said as she embraced him, and helped him peel off his school blazer.

Anna spoke up. "We passed Tibby on the street. He is on his way..."

Rick shook his head cautiously, but Marlie was hazed by the fog of her worry. "He's on his way? Oh dear... lunch. I have not made lunch. I need to go and make sure lunch is ready."

Anna stepped forward. This was something she could do. "Marlie, let me start lunch. You need to stay with Chrissy; in case she wakes up."

"Anna, I'm not sure that..."

"What were you going to serve? I can do it..." Anna insisted.

"Ma, just let us do it," said Rick firmly. "I'll help her."

"Will you? Well alright then. Finger sandwiches today. There is ham and salted beef in the meat safe and salad from the garden in the basket on the bench."

They hurried through to the kitchen, and tackled the routine, working like cogs in a machine, in the way that Marlie had drilled them when they shared the chores. Anna pulled out the loaf in the bread keeper. Rick stoked the fire to boil the kettle; sharpened the knife on a steel, to cut thin even slices of bread. Anna smeared the butter, and then they systematically prepared the toppings. Anna arranged the cut sandwiches on a china plate.

Rick watched her finish her careful arrangement of the finger sandwiches. She added some slices of cake to another plate, garnished with some fresh grapes. "You know, if nursing doesn't work out for you, we could start our own business... a café together," he said.

"Well, it would be the best little café in town."

"It would be a family affair. My schoolmaster was totally convinced you are my sister. Chrissy can bake, and you would wait the tables, because only you could persuade the customers to order more than they could possibly eat. I would wash the dishes and do the books."

"Humph. You would never do something so menial as dishes, Rick Barnes."

"That's ridiculous. I am the son of a house-steward and cook. Of course I can wash dishes."

"Your school is entirely in keeping with Grandfield, so you should do something in line with that."

He shook his head at her. "Listen to yourself Anna. You sound just like your Mother." The lunch bell tinkled. "Well, your parents are expecting lunch. You'd better scat or your alliance with the House Help will be exposed."

"I doubt it. I am supposed to be in the nursery, being tutored by Mr Weedy Meade. But he was sick this morning, so I sent him home. Hillman is probably still reading her magazines." Anna filled the teapot from the kettle and placed it on the tray to steep. Rick picked up the tray, as she disappeared back to Chrissy's room before her parents found her doing "homely" chores, which were not at all in keeping with Grandfield expectations.

* * *

Chrissy didn't improve and she didn't respond to the songs that Anna sang to her. Her coughing became more distressed. Her fever did not abate. The doctor came back again, and again, and shook his head, the line of his mouth becoming grimmer with each visit. Reverend Peters quietly sat vigil in her room with his Bible open in his lap, his lips moving silently. Tibby paced up and down praying, and praying, and praying. Chrissy's skin was hot and dry to touch. Her lips were cracked and grey, and her eyes were sunken deep, dark hollows.

After three days, the coughing stopped. The silence was deathly cold. Marlie came out of the room and took Anna in her generous arms while she screamed and screamed and screamed. Rick went outside. To which tree he sought solace, no one knew. Tibby stopped his pacing, and sat soberly in his chair, exhausted. Reverend Peters quietly closed her eyes and said more prayers.

It seemed to Anna, looking back, that this day marked the moment when the lights went out at Grandfield Park. Anna avoided Marlie and her kitchen. She was angry when Hillman told her that Marlie had brought in another girl from the neighbourhood to help her. How could she have so quickly replaced Chrissy with just anyone? She avoided Tibby except when he was driving the phaeton. She avoided Rick with his older brother tone. Nothing would ever be the same. Christmas and New Year would never be the same. It was forever grey and dark... and a little eleven-year-old girl said goodbye, not just to her friend, but to her childhood.

* * *

Part 2

Square Peg; Round Hole

1916

6.

Anna adjusted her hat and gloves one more time, as she made her way down the front steps, in the evening light. She smiled indulgently as she smoothed her shawl, and her admirer stepped forward, adjusting his army uniform jacket by the collar lapels, and gallantly offer her his arm. "You look beautiful this evening Miss Annabelle."

"Well, thank you, Henry. Be reassured my hat is well made."

He frowned and looked confused, and she waved her hand dismissively. "Don't worry, it is a private joke." Anna looked passed him to the horses and carriage standing at attention for her. She already felt bored. It seemed this outing would not serve as the distraction she had hoped. "My mission this evening is to be all attentiveness," she said with a smile, reminding herself of her assignment.

Henry glowed with anticipation. "I am delighted that you accepted my invitation."

"Well, Mother was quite insistent that I accept someone's invitation, so I guess your leave was timely."

"Then I am gratified I did not easily give up and convinced you to join me." He tucked his army hat under his arm and offered his hand to assist her up into the carriage.

Anna lifted her skirt and saw the movement of another horse leaving the stable, riding out towards the servant's gate. She recognised the familiar figure and frowned. Rick was home on leave too? She hadn't realised that. She paused to watch his easy bearing in the saddle, the smart cut of his army uniform. He pulled his mount to a halt and respectfully waited for the carriage to leave the Grandfield grounds.

Anna stared, and then as she felt his gaze rest on their party, she defiantly tilted her chin. Laughing lightly, she grabbed Henry's suspended hand. "I am delighted as well. Come, let us go or we will miss the opening aria, and that would be a tragedy so controversial that it would outdo any of the theatrical reviews of the production we are attending tonight."

As the carriage rolled slowly around the driveway, she watched Rick sitting patiently on his horse. She looked out the window and connected with his eye as they passed by. Even in the dim evening light, she could see his transparent look of... pity? Or was it disgust? And then, in a split second, she laughed with defiance and diverted her focus to the attentive Henry. "I think tonight is going to be a delightful evening. The Red Cross does such charitable work and to be amused at a time like this is indeed a consolation prize. It seems an adequate way to support their cause at the same time," she said. "I will miss you when you go away Henry. Already it seems too long." As the carriage passed through the stone gateway, she stole a look back over her shoulder. Rick was already gone.

But the evening was now spoilt. The music was rousing, the arias were magnificent, the stage settings dramatic, the theatre costumes – even in wartime, pulled from the wardrobe archives – were spectacular. But the impassioned singing was not between the star-crossed lovers on stage, or between two theatre goers seated in the gallery, but between two kids sitting in the wide branches of some sweeping camphor laurel tree talking about their future dreams. She hadn't realised that she would miss Rick. After all, she had been friends with his sister. Not him.

At intermission, an incensed Henry left Anna while he went to address the inadequate catering. Yes, there was a war on, but they were simply not getting the attention, nor the appetisers, they deserved. The matter did not disturb Anna at all. If anything, it lowered the level of boredom created by the incessant talk of war. A little reprieve from the overwhelming events that were constantly swirling around them was welcome. Anna looked around at the predominance of khaki uniforms in the various groups clustered about. Her surveillance of the room suddenly screeched to a stop as she saw Rick standing with a small group of stylish women comfortably chatting with uniformed men in their circle. Anna sighed. Men in fashionable suits were a thing of the past. The women were fanning their faces with the printed programs in their hands, laughing politely about the trivia on their lips, adeptly avoiding the fear of goodbyes. She watched curiously as Rick excused himself, and she calculated the exact time needed to intersect his path, so she could accidently bump into him as he crossed the room.

"Rick! Oh, good evening. You are here. This is a surprise."

"Anna. Good evening. Yes. I'm on a mission to find some refreshments. I suspect it might be just water tonight." He looked at her and smiled. "Some of Mum's famous lemonade would be jealously sought after just now. You could set up a stall and make a fortune. Except, I think I see Billy over there intimidating the waiters. He would probably come in and steal your takings. Should I go and apprehend him?" He directed his line of sight to where Henry was fuming at the waitstaff.

She laughed. Suddenly Rick was back, and it did her heart good. "Nope. Different bully. Well, you're in uniform, so if you do see Billy here, perhaps you would be better to deal with him directly instead of speaking in chess-code to Constable Trey." She cleared her throat. "I saw you leaving the house before. I didn't expect you were also coming here. You could have joined us."

"I doubt it. Mr Lynd would not be agreeable to that."

"Do you know Henry?" She glanced across the room where Henry's tirade was still in full force.

"We went to the same school. Even enlisted together. Don't hang out much though."

"Why would you come here? This doesn't look like the type of benefit that would interest you."

"Do not fear Anna. I am no longer your self-appointed guardian, with eyes everywhere to keep check on you. I simply promised to keep in touch with those at the office after I signed up. So, I feel obliged to try and attend some type of occasion when I am on leave. It is my hope to finish my internship when this is over. Maintaining contact is to help them not to forget me."

Oh. Was that an accusation that she had forgotten him? "I have not seen you since you enlisted. I am glad you are safe."

"Well, this might be it for a while. Our unit ships out tomorrow. Since I leave early in the morning, this is my last opportunity to make good on those promises to keep in touch."

"Why didn't you let me know you were home on leave?"

"Well, Anna Whitaker, you were obviously occupied with other matters."

"So, you asked after me?"

"Anna, you have been pretty clear that you find my company unacceptable. Perhaps I was just keeping out of your way."

"Then I am glad I bumped into you. And for the record, I find you company very acceptable. Are you enjoying the show tonight?"

"The event... sure. The company is... satisfactory." He sighed. With Anna he had always been honest. "Actually, it seems frivolous, being here... with all that is going on. But just now, it is a relief to forget for a moment. I didn't always appreciate..."

Henry bowled up and began to complain about this inadequate response to his selfless sacrifice to serve his country.

"Henry, I believe you know Richard Barnes," said Anna with her society manners neatly arranged on her lips.

Henry instinctively pulled himself up taller. "Barnes," he acknowledged, as he passed a glass to Anna. He adjusted the lapels on his jacket and glared.

Anna gasped as she heard Rick murmur in her direction. "Miss Whitaker, I believe, you were mistaken. Billy did make it tonight."

Anna coughed to cover her shock. Richard Barnes had evidently not outgrown his inclination for code. She had wondered if he would join the army as a cryptographer. That's what Max did. Decoding cyphers would be natural for him. She turned to Henry with a forced smile. "Rick was telling me his ship leaves tomorrow. I didn't realise that you may be leaving so soon as well."

"I am in a different battalion. Different roles. We have more important matters at the base to attend to first. We will be deployed in due time."

Rick raised his brow. "More important than a war?"

"Not everyone is a grunt gunner Barnes."

Anna suddenly realised she found Henry very irritating. More than Rick ever was. Perhaps all men were annoying.

Richard nodded benignly as Henry continued his sarcastic venting. Rick spoke up with an air of disinterest, without actually yawning. "Anna, it is always a pleasure. Lynd... 'til next time." And he withdrew. When she turned, Rick had already re-joined his group. The frown on Anna's brow deepened, and she turned away, mindlessly making small talk with other patrons to avoid more of Henry's incessant entitled dissatisfaction. It was a relief when they finally made their way back to the gallery, and the lights dimmed. The rest of the evening was a blur.

* * *

The thing that disturbed Anna most about the encounter with Rick at the theatre, was not the stag-fighting, head-butting, locking horns or poring the ground, as Henry Lynd tried to mark out his territory. No, it was that she had witnessed Rick's calm unwavering pursuit of his goals. Nothing was put on hold because of a world war. Not really. Even in the middle of a global crisis, he was still committed to quietly, respectfully sticking to his plan. Anna felt the sting of her own disappointed dreams. She had become her own version of what she found so irritating. Right now, the only thing she was headed for, was a betrothal into the Lynd family herd. A war-bride whose social circle mirrored her own. Did she really need to duplicate it?

Early the next morning, while the household was still quiet, and the gentle sound of Marlie stirring in the kitchen cued the morning hour, Anna went outside. She made her way through the vegetable garden that was configured like a circular maze and climbed a tree. It had been a long time since she sought solace in their branches. Perhaps she was hoping to catch a glimpse of Rick as he left through the servants' entrance to join his battalion.

But the house and grounds remained silent. As the dawn light filtered through the leaves, it shone over the garden beds. Why did she feel like she was lost in a maze without a map to get out? From this angle the configuration was rather simple. Perhaps this is why she loved being in these branches as a child. Perspective. She sat listening to the morning song of the birds. She picked a leaf and crushed it between her fingers and took a breath. The smell of dew and camphor laurel leaves surrounded her. It was peaceful here.

Anna revisited some of those blustery conversations that had occurred in these very branches when she had defended her dreams. She didn't want her words to be empty, like the large rooms in the house that echoed, hollow from the dwindling number of staff in the household. She didn't want those ambitions to come to nothing. Her dream had been to break out of the Grandfield mould. Rick had said she would never break out of her designated destiny. But it wasn't impossible... not if she wanted to. If she *really* wanted to... she could. She would.

She leant hard against the rough bark of the tree, feeling it rub against her soft skin and reflected on that thought. What did she really want? It would certainly be easier to submit to her mother's expectations and allow Henry Lynd's attentions to run their course. Her mother had said it was 'destiny', perfectly aligned in the stars. And it was true: Henry fitted the Grandfield mould so effortlessly... much better than she did herself. She wondered if she would ever really fit anywhere. She found that thought terrifying. Perhaps there wasn't a space that was her own place; somewhere that she truly felt comfortable. Was there any way she could make a significant contribution with squashing her own shape into all sorts of angles? Was that even possible in the light of the horrors of nations fighting to the death?

As she sat there, she willed her resolution to set like concrete. She knew this would be a fight, and she calmly prepared herself for the combat that this was going to unleash. The war may have opened the door of opportunity, but Anna knew she was about to bring the battle lines into her own living-room. Her mother would bunker down and resist what she was proposing to the bitter end. But Anna was determined. Rick and Pauly and Hillman were not going to be the only Grandfield residents who would contribute something meaningful to this new world in bizarre turmoil. Henry Lynd wasn't her destiny... doing something significant was. Regardless of the arguments this caused, she was determined she was not going to miss out.

* * *

7

Anna looked up as she placed her delicate breakfast cup back in its saucer. Her mother had been reading some correspondence with a frown. She screwed it up and tossed it in the fireplace. The mark on the envelope had an official look. Anna took a breath and dived in before her mother opened her next envelope.

"Mother. Mrs Lynd has inspired me to attend some charitable events... to support the war." She needed to normalise what she was doing. As her mother approved so wholeheartedly of charity and the Lynds, then combined both virtues, would be her way in.

But at the mention of Mrs Lynd's name, Evaline Whitaker immediately burred up. The implication that she might not be contributing enough when compared to her social peers, was a great insult. "Humph! What Mrs Lynd does is barely respectable. She attends some benevolent thing once a month, and perhaps during Lent and Christmas. These are times when people should focus on their family, especially when everyone's so devastated by what is going on. We already support the Red Cross, so you have no real obligation to follow Mrs Lynd's *inspiration*, just because it soothes her conscience to do so." Evaline pushed the pile of letters to the side, picked up her silver spoon and gave that look which meant the subject was closed.

Okay. Well, that didn't work. That conversation was going nowhere, so Anna determined she would just agree and then do her own thing anyway. Nothing different to what she had done her entire life really. "Oh. Of course,

Mother, you are right. I think the work you do is admirable. Yes, I am going to do that too." Anna said nothing further. And sipped her tea.

Her mother's eyes narrowed and put down her spoon. "Well, it is apparent you have already made up your mind Annabelle. What gesture of altruïsm are you going to make to support this war, when this is not really our fight anyway? You do know that some of these efforts, done in the name of charity, are less than savoury."

"I was thinking a hospital."

"A hospital? Of grief – do you have to start at the bottom? Surely you could choose something a little less... ghastly. Besides, I always make sure that we offer bric-a-brac to the hospital stalls, when they are held. And Marlie buys something when it is appropriate. And she makes biscuits to put in the home-care kits. What more could we possibly do?"

Anna blinked. Perhaps she should have started the bidding high and then wound it back. "Actually Mother, I want to be a nurse. Hillman is already graduating from a nursing school."

"No."

"What do you mean 'No'? I can serve my country if I want to."

"Anna. Nursing is not for people like us. Of course, Hillman would do that. It is completely appropriate for the help-staff.... even Marlie's kitchen maid is talking about it. But we serve our country in other, more elegant, charitable ways. Our week is already full of helpful events."

"The Auxiliary Ladies visit the wards."

"Well, the Axillary is better than nursing I suppose. What demeaning things does that entail exactly?"

"I won't know until I get there. I know some people take books... for the soldiers to read, while they are convalescing. Our Library stands neglected."

"Well, I can talk to the Chairman and have an escort arranged for you. To give you a tour. I will most likely see him in a few weeks at our community dinner."

"I trust you will have an interesting conversation then. But I have decided that I am going today," said Anna resolutely.

"Today? That's impossible! Not today."

"Today. I have planned to go there this morning."

"You can't. We are going visiting."

"That is your engagement Mother. I am not going."

"But they are expecting you."

"If they are expecting me, it is only because you told them I was coming. I never agreed."

"But it will be awkward if you don't come now. We are planning a knitting pool – to make socks. That's a very significant war contribution."

"You can simply offer my apology. I will not be missed. You carry on with your incessant planning Mother, but I am actually going to *do* something – at the hospital. I will be taking some books from our library. There are soldiers who have already been discharged from active service for medical reasons and require rehabilitating."

Suddenly her mother became very angry. She slammed her hand on the table and the china jumped and rattled in shock. "That's ridiculous! Haven't we done enough? It is preposterous that they expect us to give away our lives! It is beyond humiliating!"

Anna pushed her cup to the side and stood up. "Mother, the world has changed, and I can no longer sit by and pretend that it has stayed the same. I have asked Tibby to drop me off before you need to leave, that way your day will not be intruded upon." She walked out of the breakfast parlour with the blustery ranting of her mother falling on her back.

* * *

"Miss Whitaker, this is Mrs Bolstorff. She is the convenor of the Women's Auxiliary."

"Thank you, Sister, for bringing me here. I do want to help."

Mrs Bolstorff stood stiffly and nodded officially as the nursing sister turned on her heel in with military efficiency and left. As the door closed abruptly behind her, Mrs Bolstorff melted and turned to Anna with a soft smile. In a hushed, tired voice, she said, "I am so glad to have another in our auxiliary. You would not believe the trouble we have finding volunteers."

"I heard you lend books to the men. I have brought a selection from my father's library. I trust they will be suitable."

"There are so few staff left, that whatever we can do, helps. But still, it is hardly enough. Most of those who start in the Volunteer Auxiliary, end up doing other things to support the lads."

"Are the nurses sent away?"

"Those who are properly trained, have already gone. They are running shorter courses now, to get the basics covered. Most of the staff here are of the opinion that the Volunteer Auxiliary is made up of bored housewives who tire of their book-clubs and Red Cross fundraisers. They think we don't take the war seriously."

Anna raised her brow and wondered if Mrs Bolstorff saw her own version of restless boredom. "It seems like you take it seriously," she offered.

"My husband and son have gone to serve. I take it very seriously. But of course, being married, I cannot train as a nurse. But we can help them in their duties."

"Do they need a lot of help?"

"Yes, they do. The reality is, that there is not enough help for the job at hand." Mrs Bolstorff looked at Anna's stylish outfit, her soft hands and her manicured nails, and continued gently. "You should know that the hospital is its own private army. It has its own protocols, its own language, its own ways, its own rank and file. This is our version of the army... on the home front. It is not easy."

Anna nodded soberly. "Well, we are at war. But I am certainly keen to help, so I will enlist under you as my general."

Mrs Bolstorff's eyes glowed with approval, and she patted Anna's hand with gratitude. She showed Anna around the little room allocated to the Ladies Auxiliary. "You must have known that today is Tuesday, because our first task this morning is the patient library," she said as they loaded up a trolley with Anna's books stacked on top of the very worn volumes from the shelf. "Then we do cleaning. Just the general ward, nothing for the patients – the nurses do that." When a little mantle clock on the shelf dinged half-nine, they went to the kitchen and collected the tea trolly and pushed it out onto the ward and Anna followed with a trolly of books.

The picture Mrs Bolstorff offered was a military one. Anna preferred to think of the hospital being its own little kingdom. That appealed to the naive romance of Anna's childhood. In her games she was always able to win over the reluctant rulers and citizens, to become their beloved ambassador.

Mrs Bolstorff quietly spoke to the first patient, offered him a cup of tea, and then exchanged his book. Anna asked how he was going and struck up a conversation. Like a thirsty man holding out his cup he lapped up her words and her smile. Mrs Bolstorff indicated for them to move on. "I find it helps if we don't look at the nursing staff; just focus on the patients. And we must keep our conversations brief. The nurses don't like us to linger. We just give them their morning tea and exchange the book they took last time with a new one. They get to choose which title. Most look forward to our visits because our books offer a distraction from their plight."

As they pushed the trollies down the ward, Anna imagined she was once again in the service of King Tibby and Queen Marlie. Now she was walking through familiar territory, but this time her trolley contained important ambassadorial documents. She charmed her way into the veterans' hearts, the afflicted nodded and the infirm smiled as they received their token of distraction.

Then they did another round and collected all the mugs and delivered them to the kitchen. When they returned to the room, they stacked the books from the trolley back on the shelf and reloaded it with a bucket of water and rags. Mrs Bolstorff pegged a bag to the side of the trolly to take any rubbish. "Now we do cleaning on the ward." She showed Anna what she was to dust and wipe.

Mrs Bolstorff turned to Anna as they returned the trolley to the room. "You are a natural. I find it hard to believe you have never been in a hospital before."

Anna shrugged. "Growing up, we had private nurses when we were unwell. But I am glad can help."

At the end of the shift, she took her leave and walked outside. Anna intended to pay a cabman for her lift home, but as she passed the place where there was normally a line-up of horse-drawn Hansoms for hire, today there were no cabs waiting, so she adjusted her hat and kept walking. She went over what had been the most exhilarating morning. It was everything she imagined it would be. Anna decided that the help she offered was less about the cup of tea or book placed on their bedside cabinet, or the dusting done in the name of a clean ward, but the actual conversations she had with the patients, however short. That was the most heady of all... the way the patients responded to her. She had made a difference. Today someone had smiled because she had been there to wipe their windows-panes so their view was uninhibited with dust; tonight, someone might sleep better because of her kind words.

* * *

"You can't!" sobbed Evaline Whitaker. "This is a travesty! My son Maxwell is serving our country. You can't storm in here like an occupying army and steal away his inheritance while he is sacrificing his life for the war. This is exactly what we are fighting against. This is not appropriate at all. We are not on the war front. It is our right to stay in our home!"

The greying tones of the woman's hair seated before her, were as starched as her uniform. She sat unmoved while Mrs Whitaker shook violently in her anger. "It has been decided. Our nation is at war Ma'am, and these premises are needed. You should feel honoured to support our men in this way. They need somewhere to rehabilitate."

"Rehabilitate them somewhere else! I don't consider being invaded by occupying militia, regardless of what flag they fly, at all fortunate nor a privilege."

"You have accommodation in the Stablemaster's Lodge. That is a reasonable concession."

"Hardly reasonable at all – my groomsman lives there."

"Well... we both know that Paul Tunstall, Senior and Junior, both have enlisted. Their units have been already deployed. Mrs Tunstall has made arrangements to live with relatives inland."

"She has?"

"Yes Mrs Whitaker. You know this. You have been sent numerous notices. This cannot be a surprise to you. You have a fortnight to vacate, or you will be forcefully removed."

She gasped. "You can't!"

"We can. This is a Federally authorised war-time directive, and it states that we will be using these premises as a rehabilitation hospital. Your house staff will be given the option to stay on to support this endeavour. Consider this a demonstration of your patriotic nationalism."

"My husband is a patriot of course, but he will..."

"You are encouraged to abide by these directives in a peaceable and compliant manner, otherwise you will be seen as having treasonous leanings. Your cooperation in this matter is expected."

* * *

"Anna, I've said it before: you are a natural. Every day you walk onto the ward; the patients brighten up almost instantly." Mrs Bolstorff carefully arranged the books on the trolley according to size and subject. "The books you bring in are so appreciated by them." She paused before she spoke again. "Anna, I wonder if you have ever considered..."

"Considered... what?" Her heart leapt. What would she say?

"Well, I would not normally suggest such a thing... but like I said... you are a natural."

Anna laughed. "A natural talker? A natural people person? Others have said this before."

Mrs Bolstorff looked at her and smiled. "Well of course you are. I just wondered if you considered... well... actual nursing. I don't want to lose one of my best volunteers of course, but *imagine if* you could take your amiable nature... and add to that, some nursing skills?"

"Mrs Bolstorff? That is a very unusual thing to say." Anna shivered from the pure otherworldly nature of her question. Could she read minds?

"I only mention it because it seems obvious. I see that sort of potential in you."

"I suspect, Mrs Bolstorff, this is why you have trouble retaining your volunteers. You are boldly recruiting for active service."

"Oh, I am sorry if I spoke out of turn. I just wondered why you are content to wipe down windowsills when the patients need so much more..."

'Imagine if...', that's what Mrs Bolstorff had said. So, she did. Anna imagined what she would look like in a nursing veil. She imagined what she would look like carrying a thermometer and bandages in her pocket. And unbidden, she also imagined if she had worn a uniform the night Chrissy became sick. What a difference *that* would have made. This dream became genuinely possible.

* * *

8.

"Papa? There is something that I would ask of you."

"Annabelle? Can't it wait? We will never get through what needs to be packed away at this rate. Your mother will be back soon." He sat reading his paper and rolled his eyes in direction of the couple of staff packing.

"But I need to talk to you first."

He put down his paper and looked at his daughter cautiously through his rimless spectacles. "Are you in trouble Anna?"

"No Papa. Not at all."

"Is that Lynd boy treating you well? I am surprised you are not engaged yet. Many of the boys find that an encouragement... knowing their girl is at home waiting for them."

"This is not about Henry. Papa, I think that...well, what I wish to speak of, will be hard for you to accept. But I want you to know that this is something that I have considered very seriously."

Just then her mother walked through the door. Anna sighed. Her moment was taken.

Her mother threw her gloves on the sideboard and her hands in the air. "These people are absolutely fickle! They could not make up their mind about whether it should be Spring or Autumn. Then, just as we determined our preference, someone pipes in with *Winter*. Winter! My goodness. *Just make a decision*, I said to them. And still they wavered. It amazes me how they are able to even dress themselves! If it was not for me, we would still be debating the ins and outs of it."

"Then it is a good thing you were there My Dear," said her father soothingly. "What do you think we should do with the linen? I had hoped you would stay and help here. We have so little time."

"They expect me to put my life on hold and do something as unreasonable as living in a worker's cottage! Being at the committee feels slightly more normal than everything else that is happening here. You and Tibbs are managing fine."

"Linen?" he repeated with raised eyebrows.

"Well, I suppose they will need some of it. Keep the best sets for the lodge." She looked around and saw Anna. "Did I interrupt something?"

"No. Not really Mother."

"Annabelle said there was something that she wanted to talk to us about. Something important," said her father.

Anna internally groaned. This was not how her strategy played out in her mind.

"Really? Have you decided on what things to pack away as well? I have Tibbs putting our best antique furniture pieces into storage. Some of those pieces are your inheritance."

"Mother, I have done what you have asked, but I am seriously considering packing up in another sense. This is what I wanted to discuss. I..."

"Oh? Well, that is something. I am gratified that you are taking the initiative on these important matters Annabelle. At some point you will be the mistress of your own home. When this war is over you will need to be able to operate independently. I will not always be here, at your beck-and-call."

The idea of her mother being at anyone's beck-and-call was distracting. Anna took a breath, focused, and launched in. "When you move,

I will be moving into the nurse's quarters at the hospital. You will find living in Tunstall's house quite restrictive, and this works well because I have applied to train to become a nurse." She still needed the forms signed, but in her mind, it was already done.

The room went still. Then her mother burst out laughing. "Oh my! You say the funniest things, Annabelle. I thought you had given up on that ridiculous notion! Now, we do have a couple of guests coming this evening, so try and think of something more suitable to wear than a nurses' veil and cape." Her mother went and poured herself a drink from the cabinet, chuckling. "Oh my. A nurse. I never."

Anna pasted on a smile, and nodded, and left the room. Her mother's denial of reality never ceased to frustrate her. She went out the back and walked around the herb garden centred around Marlie's lemon tree. She picked some sage and rubbed it between her fingers as she wandered past the Glasshouse, packed full of seedlings. These would be needed for the hospital vegetable garden now. Everything pointed towards the hospital. Grandfield Park no longer existed. She touched the textured bark of the trunks of the camphor laurel trees that were no longer climbed; she wandered into the grounds. Anna found herself down in Chrissy's little alcove. This was the place where once her dreams were believable and achievable. Where nothing was impossible, where the insurmountable was never too hard.

"I can do this. I can do this... and if I can't... I can do all things through Christ who strengthens me." That mantra was something that Marlie used to say, but she really preferred to have confidence in her own autonomy. "*I* can do this." She took a breath and reminded herself of all the reasons why pursuing this was a worthy thing. Perhaps after her training she could come back and work on staff at this rehabilitation hospital. Without any conscious thought, one motivating thought was that she wanted to prove to Richard that she was not just a talker... not just a planner. She imagined telling him that she had accomplished real things too. Serious things. This idea became a driving force, pushing her forward. "Yes! I can do this."

* * *

"Papa?"

He looked up from packing away some of his records with the startled look of a rabbit being cornered into a fence. "Your mother is not back yet."

"I know. But..."

"Surely you are not going to ask about that... again?"

"Yes, I am. I need to know if you have signed the forms we talked about. I know you are busy, but I have mentioned this many times. Father, you are being evasive. You need to sign it. Where did you put the paperwork, Papa?"

"Anna. Annabelle. You know what your mother has said. She is not willing to entertain the notion."

"I know... which is why I am talking with you. You understand me, Papa. You know I will not be satisfied with being just another Mrs Lynd. I have more inside of me Papa. You know I have more."

"Oh Anna, my Belle.... I know. But a nurse? Isn't it enough that you are on the hospital auxiliary. They do such crude and ungainly work. And now they are going to turn our beautiful home into a place of suffering and death. It doesn't bear thinking about! It is not right that my daughter would work in her family home as a nurse."

"It could be a place of healing and life. I still require training, regardless of where I work." Anna went over and kissed her father's cheek. This was progress. It was no longer a flat out 'No'.

Anna doggedly jumped all the hurdles she needed to follow this course to the end. She begged and cajoled her father to sign those papers. She pursued him relentlessly until he put his name on the form, all be it reluctantly.

Her father had signed the paper, confident it would not take long for this latest whim to be out of Annabelle's system, and then she could come home, and their life could resume 'normal'... even if that 'normal' was completely abnormal, living in the stable-hand's cottage.

When her mother found out what had been done, she screamed and yelled. Evaline Whitaker declared she would disown Anna if she persisted with these frivolous notions. When she had sufficiently calmed, Mrs Whitaker demanded that Anna offer sufficient reassurances that she would not tell anyone about this irrational phase she was going through. In addition to that, Anna had to vow on her life that she would never come back and work in her family home as a "hospital nurse" ... staff... a dogsbody... a handmaiden emptying night-soil.

Anna moved into the nurses' quarters; at the same time her mother and father moved into the Stablemaster's Lodge. The humiliation drove her mother underground. She never wrote to Anna; she never replied to any of the notes that Anna mailed. Anna had emphatically made this bed... all be it a very sterile, severe, hard hospital bed... and now she was obliged to lie in it. Alone.

* * *

9

They stood around the heavy metal bed in the nursing schoolroom; their serge uniforms were starched and stiff. This was war. Here they started their journey to learn nursing care, first aid, hospital sanitation, as well as other matters that Anna had strictly attributed to soldiers: the use of gas masks, camouflage techniques, and map reading. They were also required to attend physical training. Australian nurses had a reputation for gritty excellence and determination. But active service required a full graduating qualification. This was a standard at Anna aspired to attain.

Back to the bed. Making a bed was deemed as the first and foundational lesson in nursing school. Anna stared at the tall iron bed and was shocked to learn that 'Making a bed' was the lynch pin of nursing practice. She had anticipated something much more... more like healing. Bandaging wounds perhaps. But no. Obviously not. Here she was, staring at a stark iron bedframe. The nursing sister paused to gather her breath, before she launched into her rationale for making a bed properly and well. "This is how you make a bed. This is the only way to make a bed. There are to be no creative versions of this. It is done this way and only this way. At all times. Our soldiers depend on it."

She spoke like a gatling gun, emphasising every second word, spital splattering the atmosphere around her. Anna instinctively stepped back and thought of Mrs Bolstorff's description of the hospital army. That would make Sister Perry the gunner's sergeant. When the demonstration was finished, the starched folds of the sheets were crisp, folded like plated metal.

Then it was their turn. Anna frowned as she looked around the group. It was strange that their names had all been taken away. Now they were only addressed as 'Nurse'. Her badge labelled her as 'Nurse'. Not Nurse Anna. Not Nurse Whitaker. 'Nurse'. She was partnered with a young nurse with brown hair whose name was also Nurse. "What is your name?" Anna whispered to Nurse.

She turned away and focused intensely on folding cardboard corners over the mattress.

"What's your name?" Anna repeated.

"Ellie," she whispered impatiently.

"Ellie? Is that short for something?"

"Elspeth. Shh. You'll get me in trouble."

Elspeth reminded Anna of a puppy, enthusiastically wagging her tail, waiting for a treat to be toilet trained. Perhaps it was not by mistake that they called this drill, 'nursing training'. Then she sighed. Anna remembered Richard pouring over his books. They train dogs, but she had enrolled hoping for an *education*.

Then there was the lesson on how to clean the bedside lockers. Only specific items were allowed on the bedside cabinet, regimented, lined up in military formation. The lines on the towels were even as they hung on the rail, neat and symmetrical. With systematic and military efficiency their lessons continued. Cleaning and cleaning and cleaning.

There was no delay in putting these newly acquired skills on the wards. Probational students were required to put in a full day's work... and then some. For Anna making beds and cleaning was hardly different to the Women's Auxiliary. But... then, it was different. Here they did not have the liberty to smile and chat. They followed the nursing sister onto the ward, marching in formation like a military troop. Anna looked into the faces of the patients as they marched passed, and she smiled and nodded to some of the familiar characters who had gratefully taken books from her hands. But there was no recognition, only their eyes were curious as to what the 'new' nurses looked like: fresh faces, with new aprons tied around their heavy surge uniforms, with bibs and capes and caps. A few of the men responded with a wink, but otherwise they stayed neutral.

They were taken into a long ward, and one by one the beds were emptied of their patients. Anna buddied up with Nurse Elspeth as they began to make real beds for real patients, while the patient sat in his cold iron-framed upright chair. Anna looked reassuringly at her partner as they stripped the bed. "Don't worry, I used to volunteer for the Auxiliary. I've seen this done a thousand times. What do you think about our first day?" she whispered to Nurse Elspeth.

"I feel like we are straight into doing nursing," she whispered back. "I thought it would take longer to get into it."

"Nurse! No time to chat. You are not here to have tea and scones. Get to work! Show me you can make a bed properly like a nurse."

Ellie blushed bright red, ducked her head and quickly returned to her starched sheets.

Anna shrugged and kept turning down sheets. She could not see that they had done anything that warranted embarrassment. Sister Perry marched along the end of the beds barking out instructions to her novices. She passed them and then came back and stared at their bed. Anna looked up at her buoyantly. "How are we doing Sister?" she asked hopefully.

Sister shook her head and pursed her lips in disgust. She said nothing but reached down and stripped the bed in a single sweep of her hand. "Do it again. And do it properly this time!"

Every bed they made that morning was given the same treatment. Just as they were adding a blanket, Sister Perry swooped in and stripped back the bed to the mattress, and they had to start again.

As Anna folded the sheets in starched cardboard folds again, she turned to the patient with a hopeful twist of her lips. Perhaps his bed might now be suitably made. An older nurse pushed her to the side. "Get out of my way," she growled. "I need to help my patient back into bed."

Anna stumbled, shocked by her rudeness. "How dare you!" she said burring up. The nurse turned to her and said very quietly, "Who is daring who, Nurse?" Anna was ready to spit out the retort on her tongue, when Sister Perry appeared like an apparition with a deep scowl on her face. Anna hesitated and took a breath, swallowing her pride and her comments. She was learning to nod and move on to the next bed that needed to be stripped and made... and more often than not... remade, more than twice at Sister Perry's command.

* * *

The next day, they were promoted to cleaning the patients. "This is how you deliver a bedpan. This is the only way to deliver a bedpan. There are to be no creative versions of this. It is done this way and only this way, at all times." They went through the fifty-six steps that were entailed in completing this complex nursing task. Select the pan; warm the pan; dry the pan; cover the pan with a starched linen cover; hold the pan just so; position the screens; use a modesty cloth; remove the sheets; roll the patient; assist the positioning; turn away for privacy... etcetera, etcetera, etcetera.

"This is the way you roll a bandage. This is the only way to roll a bandage. There are to be no creative versions of this. It is done this way, and only this way, at all times." Then there were hours and hours of sorting through the table piled high with knotted, tangled bandages, that looked like a giant bowl of Italian spaghetti. They were set to work, smoothing, and rolling, and stacking in various boxes according to the size of rolled bandages.

Anna had hoped that Nurse Elspeth would become an ally in this battlefield of training. But Ellie quickly learnt to partner with one of the other nurses if she was going to get her work done without having to redo it at least twice. Even during the breaks, she avoided her.

"Why don't you want to work with me?" Anna asked Ellie directly one day as she sat down beside her in the dining room. Anna screwed up her face at the tepid tea and tried to eat the mushed shepherds' pie that was more accurately warmed gravy smeared with a thin layer of watery potato slop.

"I don't know what you mean," Ellie said evasively.

"Yes, you do. You are avoiding me."

"Well, it just so happens that I remember you, Anna Whitaker. But it seems that you have no recollection of me at all."

"We've met? But that's good, isn't it? When...?"

"See... I don't think you understand. *You* used to avoid *me*. You didn't even notice who I was back then because I didn't fit your snobby ideas. Well, fortunately for me, snobby doesn't get any points here, only very well-made beds. Which you don't seem to be able to manage. You are like a cursed penny Anna. Sister Perry always makes you redo everything. I need to protect my progress. Nothing personal." It sure felt personal. The other students had consistently objected when they were partnered with Anna as well, until she felt like a leper. Never before, in her entire protected life, had Anna experienced the pain of exclusion.

* * *

Sister Perry cleared her throat before she launched into the next lesson. "This is how you do a sponge bath. This is the only way to sponge a patient. There are to be no creative versions of this. It is done this way, and only this way, at all times. Our soldiers depend on it."

There was a wooden mannequin in the practice bed, and Sister Perry went through the ritual of sponging this immobile lump of wood. Anna blushed as it was stripped naked and covered in towels. Limb by limb, section by section, the body was sponged and dried. Then they were to attend to the groin area. "Oh no. I don't think I can do that," Anna said modestly as she was handed the washer.

"Don't be bashful Nurse. Anatomy is as natural as the hair on our head. Just get to it."

"But..."

"Do it. Now! You wash your own body, don't you? This afternoon we do real bodies, in real beds, on a real ward. You will need to do it then, so you start now. You do it this way, or you will be the humiliation of our very noble Hospital and our very noble Nursing School. Hurry up."

* * *

"Nurse! Don't just stand there. You have been told what to do. You need to attend to this patient and do it quick smart." The Ward Sister glared at her in a steely gaze.

"Yes Sister." Anna wiped her clammy hands down her apron and swallowed. This man was angry. Very angry. Any attempts to help him, was received by him spitting out vile profanities. Yet Anna had been allocated to attend to this man... every shift. But she was pretty sure it was more than the bad luck of drawing the short straw each shift.

"Nurse! Don't be tardy. If you need to wipe your hands, do it on a towel, after you have washed them with soap and water. Not on your apron. Now go and wash them – again. Now!"

"Yes Sister."

Later that morning, Sister Perry pulled her aside. "Listen to me Nurse. This has gone on too long and I need to address it. Don't think for a second that your name, your mother or your money means anything in here. You will get no special privileges just because you are a Whitaker, or because your parents have associates on the Hospital Board. Not from me, not from anyone else that matters. No one at all. I will see to it. You will do exactly what every other nurse must do. Do you understand?"

"Yes Sister."

"See, I don't think you understand at all. If you think for a second it will prove anything to have a particular home address in here, you have a second think coming. There is a war on, and that is the ultimate leveller... especially here... except for you. You are on the bottom rung. And the ladder of the probationary student nurse stands tall against the wall of the grand tradition of our hospital. You insult it just by being here!"

"But Sister... I..."

"Don't sass me, Nurse! Go into the sluice room and scrub it until it shines like new penny. I will be in, in two minutes to check up on you." Sister Perry turned on her heel and stomped down the hall, her hard heels clunking like the drum of a military band.

Sister Perry did her inspection as she vehemently declared. She came in with a white glove and ran her fingertip around the top rim of the skirting board. She inspected the smudge her index finger and stared at Anna in disgust. "As predicted, you are wasting our resources, you careless, spoilt little brat! It's wartime! We have to be frugal with every penny. Having you here costs money. Our men are away fighting for our nation and all you can do is stand there stammering that you have tried your best. Well, your best is not good enough! Now do it again until it is right!" She was determined that Anna would fail, and her mission was to send her cowering back to her corner of the Stablemaster's residence on Parkland Avenue. It was beyond Sister Perry's comprehension that Anna had not already quit. Because of her name she could not fail her, but she could surely make certain Nurse Whitaker left on her own volition.

Anna trembled under the disfavour. What had she done to offend her so thoroughly? None of it made sense. But as Anna gasped and tried to hold it together, leaning over the bench, she dried her eyes and washed her hands again, and tried to ignore the chaffing on her fingers as she dried them on the hard towels. She tipped out a small portion of cleaning powder on the bench and started to scrub the instruments lined up there, until they shone like Tibby's silver. This sudden intimacy with body waste and biological fluids made Anna's stomach churn. Another nurse came in and dumped a pile of soiled linen on the floor and threw out an explanation over her shoulder as she dashed away. The stench caused Anna to retch into the sink. She wiped her face and went back to work.

This was her lot every day. The other nurses that Anna started with, including Ellie, progressed through their levels quickly. Yet Anna remained scrubbing pans in the sluice room. Sister Perry made sure that she had become the object of every Ward Sister's scrutiny. Try as she might, her work never measured up to their exacting standards. Where were the patients in all of this? Weren't the patients supposed to be the point of this? Staff referred to the leg injury in Bed Four, and the fever in Bed Twelve, the burns isolated in Bed Eighteen and the diarrhoea and vomiting in Bed Twenty-three. Names, and identities, and the humanness of this place was swallowed up in procedures, meagre resources, a monster that fed on suffering, injury and sickness.

If Anna had not been another body who wore a uniform, and another hand which held a thermometer in a dwindling wartime workforce, she knew they would have dismissed her long ago. Even though she did well enough in her lessons, this became just another point of failure. "If you can answer the questions on paper Nurse, then surely you can do it on the ward. If not, you need to go back to where you have come from."

That was the consistent message: *you don't belong here.* Anna shivered in horror as she went on with scrubbing porcelain bed pans, whimpering at the weeping fissures between her fingers. But she could not go home. She had burnt that bridge. Bombed it, actually. The war was a reality every day of her life, and she was firmly in the middle of enemy territory. All the street signs had been taken down, the bridges had all been taken out, the night sky was blacked out, and there was no way back and no way forward.

Her mother had told her that a global war was not a reasonable excuse to put on a nurses' cap. When she chose this path, she had sealed her fate and was not welcome back. The morning Anna left home, her mother told her in no uncertain terms she was abandoning her heritage, her future, especially her mother. The Whitaker name would never recover from the shame that was inflicted on it because they were forced to move into the Stablemaster's residence. And somehow this was all Anna's fault. Her father insisted everyone agreed the rehabilitation hospital was unrealistic. If they can't staff existing hospitals, why create more. There was even talk of an orphanage when the war was over. Again – unnecessary. New families could be found when those deployed came home. Anna's nursing enrolment was just another ridiculous outcome of a world overreacting, especially when everything would be over by the end of the year anyway. But they said that last year... and there was no indication that those hopeful projections were any closer to being fulfilled.

* * *

10

The notion, the idealism, the fanciful impression of what nursing would be like, was obliterated now. But the system had its tentacles around Anna so tightly, that there was no escape. When Anna wrote to Henry about her decision to enlist in the war effort by becoming a nurse, she at least expected some support from the idea that she was fighting the same war alongside him. His response was definite. "Anna! You shouldn't have done that! It is right that you stay home and wait for me. That's what other women do. You should too."

Anna disagreed. Women did all sorts of things to contribute. So, when Anna postponed Henry's urgent proposal on his final leave before he was deployed overseas his frustration turned to fury. When she persisted in resisting his attempts to put a ring on her finger when he wrote to her, he refused to correspond with her. By insisting on choosing nursing, she had taken marriage off the table. Initially the space from his criticism was a relief. But as the loneliness set in, she started to crave his self-absorbed accounts of all his achievements. She told herself that he was entitled to a connection at home, given the scope of what he was going through. His throw-away compliments during their previous dates now felt sincere in the face of the constant criticism Anna was bombarded with, so she relented on her resolve to withdraw, and wrote Henry a letter. Well, maybe a few letters. But not one of those letters were answered. She stopped writing when she read in the newspaper social column that the society belle Margaret Munnerlyn – one of her long-time 'snobby and rude' childhood friends, was the focus of Henry Lynd's attentions. Another newspaper article reported the announcement of Margaret's engagement to Henry. The story was written as a romantic piece.

War brides doing their bit for the cause: knitting socks at home as a warm gesture of their faithfulness to their men and country. Anna didn't really know what to feel when she read that. That *could* have been her, *should* have been her. If she had listened to her mother, it *would* have been her. As she stared at the sketched illustration in the newspaper of a blushing bride-to-be, holding her knitting needles attached to a half-made pair of socks, reading the letter that penned her proposal, Anna wondered if this nursing life, which she had fought so hard to experience, was worth it. Was this really the significant, commendable, bigger thing she was destined for? It didn't seem like it. But perhaps this was her version of the front line. So, she wrote to Max instead. She peeled off her thick stockings mended with darned patches, at the end of her shift, and rubbed her aching feet with lotion. She wrapped her cracked, bleeding hands in bandages and cotton gloves, and tried to read something less horrifying than newspaper articles, until the book fell from her bandaged hands, and she fell asleep.

In all of this horror, Marlie's letters came like a trickle of life-giving water. They were always short and kind. Anna replied to every single one. She sanitised her account of nursing life in her letters. With the articulate poise, she would clean up her reports just like she would scrub away the soil from the emesis bowls on the ward. Even this exercise helped her survive. She had to filter through the drudgery and pointlessness of her shifts to find flecks of quartz in the silt. Anna no longer hoped that this mental fossicking would ever find anything as worthy as gems. Just a shiny piece of worthless quartz in the sludge would be enough.

"I have a patient who smiles at me every day. I take particular care when I make his bed, because he has no family to visit him, and it is a way I can chat with him just a few moments more. There was lady, in the female surgical section. If I am working late, and there are no other staff around, I

make sure I go to her bed and hold her hand and wish her good night, and then we whisper a prayer together."

Anna looked at what she had written and sighed. These flecks of quartz were rare and precious. There was always someone supervising her closely, because she could not be trusted to do her work well enough, or fast enough. There were always someone telling her that *she* didn't belong.

* * *

After one long night shift, as the sun was rising, Anna went to Women's Volunteers Auxiliary office to see Mrs Bolstorff. She sat in the room, in the early morning stillness, waiting for her to bundle into the room with her warm shawl and her warm smile. Anna thought that perhaps if she could just talk with her again, she would be reassured that she had done the right thing... a worthy thing. After all, Mrs Bolstorff was the one who had encouraged her with that tantalizing invitation to *"imagine if..."*

But it was not Mrs Bolstorff who came through the door. Another woman stood there, cold and stern. Her face was covered with a shawl, wrapped around her nose and mouth with only her eyes showing, as a precaution against influenza. If the war was not enough, the dreaded Spanish Flu had piled fear on top of fear, death on top of death.

Anna smiled. She had seen Mrs Bolstorff with that same severe look when they first met. But this woman's eyes never softened, they just stared at her nurse's uniform. "You shouldn't be here. Is it not enough that you nurses run everything else in this hell-hole?"

"Mrs Bolstorff was my friend. I came to see how she was."

"I wouldn't be publishing your affections for that quarter young lady. That woman was a kraut, and she had no right being here."

"That's rubbish! Mrs Bolstorff worked her heart out for this place. Her husband and son enlisted to serve our country," declared Anna, fiercely loyal.

"That is doubtful. Hun with a *boche* name. They will always align with the enemy. She was taken into custody as a spy... not that you heard that from me."

"A spy! That's impossible!"

"Humph! Impossible it certainly isn't. And I heard those camps all caught the Spanish flu. Ironic... but natural justice I would say."

Anna gasped. "Interned... with the Flu? But who is looking after them?"

"Who knows? You are a nurse. That's your job. She won't be coming back here, that is for certain."

"I need to go ..."

"You do that." She stood stiffly by the open door, and Anna fled.

It was not until she was in the nurses' quarters, locked up in her cell, that Anna finally let her tears fall in a hysterical, heated mess. Even kind Mrs Bolstorff had succumbed to the injustice of a world broken by war, and injury, and disease, and hate. There was no hope for such a place.

* * *

Part 3

The Shape of Me

1919

Anna sat in the shadows of a small teahouse that was not far from Grandfield; her coat draped over the chair beside her. An older woman shuffled past, her old-fashioned skirt swishing in hushed whispers across the floor. Women usually wore shorter skirts now-a-days. A gentleman tipped his hat as she passed. But Anna noticed nothing of that. Her eyes were focused on the door, the bright morning light causing splashes of white against her lids when she blinked. Her face was wrapped up in a shawl – the manner of covering their faces was becoming more common as the cases of the Spanish flu rose.

She slipped aside her scarf and drank from the glass of water nervously. Had he received her message?

Suddenly he was standing beside her table. "Miss Anna?"

"Oh Tibby! You came!" She looked around and covered her face again, in case someone recognised her. "Sit down. Please."

He sat comfortably, his grey eyes drinking in the sight of her. Strands of long hair that escaped her shawl, were dull and lacklustre. Even though her face was covered in the cowl, he could tell her naturally thin face looked gaunt. "Oh Miss Anna. It is good to see you."

"Oh Tibby – I don't know what I would have done if you hadn't come."

"Wild horses wouldn't have kept me away Miss Anna. You know that."

She smiled wearily, out of relief. "I know."

"These have been a long couple of years," he said as he took off his driving gloves and laid them beside his hat.

"Three years, five months, two weeks and four days." And she unwrapped her mask as her teacup and pot was put on the table. "But who's counting?" Her eyes blinked hard as she lifted a gloved hand to detain the waiter. "Tea, black, half a sugar... Thanks."

"No sugar without a coupon Miss," the waiter said.

"You want a whole coupon for half a teaspoon of sugar? Oh come on! The war is over."

"Restrictions haven't been lifted yet Ma'am..."

"Plain, black is fine," said Tibbs, gently raising his hand. "I have adjusted, Miss Anna... but it is nice that you have not forgotten."

"Forgotten? I made it too many times to forget! It is burnt into my soul."

"Your mother would be horrified if she knew we let you make real tea with hot water," he said with a gentle smile. Images of Anna and Chrissy playing tea parties in their lounge room, appeared unbidden and he swallowed the lump in his throat. Anna always insisted that they use a china teapot with real tealeaves, and Chrissy would fuss as he sat at a small chopped down table, sipping their tarry concoctions as if it was nectar from heaven.

"How's Marlie?"

"She's well... and as beautiful as ever."

"Oh Tibby – you old romantic!" It occurred to Anna in that moment that perhaps her reluctance to marry Henry Lynd it was less about escaping the life set by her parents, or the impossible standards of the society Lynds... perhaps it was also about pursuing something better that this couple had modelled. Had the servants at Grandfield quietly instilled in her a desire for grander possibilities? It was Tibby and Marlie who had set this romantic bar so high. "And Rick? Have you heard from him?"

"We only get a little correspondence of course, and his letters still have large blocks of writing redacted. They look like a chequerboard with so much blacked out, but it seems he'll be discharged soon. He's very hopeful he will get his old position back at the firm." He sighed and put down his cup. "Miss Anna – what is it? You didn't send for me to update on our family's health. How are you really? You look tired." The dark circles under her gaunt eyes did not look tired; they were the mark of exhaustion. Did she even have the right to be tired, when the horror of the front lines was filtering back, telling of a nightmare that was not going away... even when the war was over.

"It's hard work ..." and although she thought she had no more tears to shed, they welled up. She thought when war was over, that would be her reprieve, but then the wards were overwhelmed again from the influx of patients with the Spanish Flu. How could Noah ever hope the world would recover from so many floods?

Tibby waited, searching her face with concern. "If I know you Miss Anna, hard work is not the problem. You are very determined."

"Oh Tibby!" The tears fell freely now. She picked up a serviette and dabbed at the dark circles impatiently.

Tibby noticed the disregard of etiquette wordlessly. More than a few things had changed.

"I wanted to help so badly! But it was not at all what I thought! I can't do it anymore!" There. It was out. She had succumbed to failure. As soon as she was able, it was a relief to close the door on nursing and leave it behind.

"You could come home Miss," he suggested quietly.

"Oh, Tibby. No! You know I couldn't... not yet. I need time. Mother would never..."

He patted her hands in a gesture of fatherly reassurance. She winced and recoiled, dropping them in her lap.

"Anna? Show me your hands," he said quietly and firmly.

The gentle authority in his voice was comforting. She swallowed and reluctantly rested her hands on the table. He turned her gloves over and noticed her grimace in pain. He could see the lines of bandages and the stains of dark ooze penetrating through the wadding.

He stood abruptly. "You are coming home. Marlie will see to this." He gathered her coat, guiding her by the elbow to a small, buggy with a canopy waiting outside. For once in her life Anna didn't object.

* * *

Spreading camphor laurel trees dappled shafts of light on the driveway as they drove past the imposing stone gates of Grandfield Park, to the service entrance. "Just keep your head down Miss. Your mother is coming," Tibby said with the calm disregard of delivering a weather report.

Anna groaned audibly and shrank back into the shadows. He went to drive directly towards the stables, but the tall dominating profile of her mother stepped fearlessly in front of the buggy.

Tibby pulled to a halt, and the horse threw back his head. He leaned forward, adjusting his hat against the glare. "Ma'am?"

"Tibbs! Where have you been?"

"Just collecting a family friend Mrs Whitaker," he said looking straight ahead.

Evaline snorted and glanced into the dark shadows of the covered canvas. The plain brown travel coat and nondescript hat didn't interest her.

"You don't have time for a personal life today, Tibbs. There is a myriad of things to be done! We barely have five hours before our guests start arriving for the Benefit. Every time another batch of our dear boys come home it is incumbent that we show our appreciation. It is a relief to be able to observe our regard again... and it is our responsibility to celebrate our triumph. You know how important this is. Come around to the Glasshouse immediately!"

She kept her eyes down as her mother's definite footfall faded on the gravel driveway. The wheels turned slowly again.

"Tibby, why is Mother still ordering you around? Aren't you employed by the Hospital now? And why is she so interested in the Glasshouse? It doesn't seem likely she has suddenly developed a passion for gardening. She only goes near that place when the orchids were in bloom."

He chuckled. "Actually, all the orchids have gone. They have made a small shade house for the soldiers to look after some pot plants that they rotate through the wards. The curators have given consent for your Mother to transform the Glasshouse into a ballroom to hold her fundraisers... for our hospital and returned servicemen. She is being recognised for making a significant contribution to the recovery effort."

Anna closed her eyes and shook her head. Of course she was. Mother was very happy to own the war when it involved a party. "Thank you, Tibby... for not..."

"Hush Child. Marlie will get you some breakfast," he said, as he bundled her quietly through the door, and Anna collapsed sobbing into the open arms of Marlie.

* * *

For three restless weeks Anna slept. When she woke Marlie would bathe the deep red, weeping fissures on her hands and then dress them. She applied a concoction made from her grandmother's recipe using a base of cod-liver-oil. Unfortunately, although the remedy was effective, the ointment smelt like dead fish which had feasted on rotted potatoes. Anna did not object – it was no worse than three years of doing laundry, soiled from any combination of body-fluids. Marlie would apologetically wrap Anna's hands gently in clean bandages and then she would flop back between fresh sheets.

They smuggled a doctor in from the hospital wards, through the servants' entrance. He wrote out a prescription for a less offensive salve. Marlie had Tibby take her down to see the druggist, Mr Errol Grimes, to have the prescription made up. The first thing Anna did was buy some lavender water. Grimes was mortified by the state of her hands. But he agreed with the doctor that it was not just her hands that needed healing, so he also made up a tonic, and prescribed more rest. Lots of rest.

Marlie was loyal to her grandmother's balm. She declared the concoction had never failed her yet. Anna decided to test it by getting Marlie to dress one hand with the doctor's prescription and the other with her homemade remedy. Within the week they could clearly see Marlie's salve was getting better results, so Anna covered her nose, slathered on the lavender water, and slept and slept.

"The poor little Mite's beyond exhausted Tibby," said Marlie one night after the clean up after dinner was finished. "One wouldn't let a dog get into such a state. It's inhuman." Marlie's hair, sprinkled with grey, was tied in a bun at the nape of her neck. Her generous bosom heaved. "Tiberius you must tell them."

"Now Marlie don't start. You know I cannot. Not until she says."

"But they're her parents. Oh Tibs... if this was Chrissy, I wouldn't abide it. If someone knew she was here and didn't tell me. Families should be together..." Marlie sat down heavily. She only alluded to Chrissy when things weighed heavily on her heart. Fractured families were everywhere... in every street... every house. Rarely did they get the privilege of being reunited. These past months had been the worst. When the hope of peace soars, the telegrams of loss seem darker. Tibbs came over and laid a hand on her shoulder. "God have mercy on us Tibs. We shouldn't be doing this," she said with a sigh.

"Now Marlie, you're forgetting two things. Miss Anna is a grown woman who can make her own choices. She has always known her own mind and this is what she wants. And two, Mrs Whitaker has asserted many times that when Anna left, she wiped her hands of her unruly ways."

"Unruly my foot! The girl's got a heart the size of an ocean-going steamship."

"Very true, Marlie. Her ship has seen rough seas. She needs the shelter of a safe harbour. She needs your loving touch Marlie."

She sighed again as she looked at her husband. She never doubted his wisdom, but when it came to Anna, he had always been a little unreasonable. Anna and Chrissy were... She didn't finish the thought. Even now it was tender to touch. The layer of years had not wiped away the pain. She loved Anna – as her own daughter. Her other daughter. Marlie sighed and drifted off to bed.

Tiberius placed a log on the fire. He sat down in his chair and opened his Bible. Maybe Marlie was right. Perhaps he should tell her father. But Mr Whitaker would be obliged to tell his wife, and that thought sent a shudder down his spine. The girl didn't need an inventory of wrongs. She needed love and care. Just because the Whitakers had moved out of the main residence into the coach-house, it did nothing to shift their commitment to the old order.

If change was part of what they had been fighting for, it was wasted effort in this little corner of Grandfield. He looked at the words before him and they seemed to swim around the page, except one line. *"Whoever receives one of these little children in my name receives me..."* The words of Jesus soothed his nettled conscience. Anna's wishes came first. Tiberius closed his eyes and breathed a prayer.

He opened his eyes and saw Anna standing at the open door with a shawl wrapped around her shoulders. She shivered in the night air. "Sorry. Am I disturbing you?" she whispered apologetically.

"Not at all Miss Anna." He quickly got up and stirred the fire.

"Tibby? Could I ask something of you?"

"Certainly Miss Anna."

"Please drop the 'Miss'. You have known me forever. I'm staying as a guest in your home."

"Old habits die hard Miss Anna. But I will try if you like."

"Yes, I like... very much." She sighed and curled up on the settee, wrapping a rug around her legs. "You and Marlie are so kind. Thank you for not telling on me." She sounded like a child again.

"And how do you know that we haven't?"

Anna laughed softly and shook her head. "Because I'm still here..."

"Oh Miss Anna... Anna, it is music to hear you sound more like your old self. Marlie has been beside herself with worry."

Anna sobered and said nothing for a while. "Tibby? How could I have been so wrong?"

"About what?"

"About nursing. I fought tooth and nail to go – and Mother never approved. I twisted my father's arm to sign the papers. I can't bear the thought that Mother was right, and yet... it is true... it was completely horrible. Every moment! I kept hoping it would be better – that it would begin to be more what I hoped... but it never did. It just didn't!" She was angry. She had been lied to... even if it was by her own fanciful naivety. Anna looked at her wrapped hands bandaged in Marlie's homemade salve and clean linen.

"I never understood why you didn't come and work here. I thought it might have been better, working in the house you know, close to those you love, supporting the..."

"I wanted to. But Father only agreed to sign if I vowed never put my mother in the position of having to face the humiliation of her daughter on staff here. At the time I thought it was the cost of a dream. But it..."

"Do you want to talk about it?"

"What can I say?" She shrugged. At loss for words.

Tibby said nothing but got up and came back with a tea tray. He passed her a china cup and a chipped saucer.

"Tibby..." Anna paused. Her voice was tense, full of emotion. She had been so resolved that nursing would be her significant thing. That was supposed to be her destiny.

"You've had a bad time of it, Anna."

"But it was never meant to just be a war thing. It was supposed to be my life work... my 'significant thing'. The war was my way in. But when I got there, I couldn't wait for a way out. Even now, with so much need from the Spanish flu, it no longer seems like a good enough reason to stay. Am I so deficient? I tried so hard Tibby! I truly did."

"I would say you did stick it out. Maybe it was just not for you. Perhaps it was the ideal that appealed to you... or perhaps the translation of it was stolen by the war and the people over you, so you never got to experience it the way it was meant to be."

"Not once did I feel like I made a difference. I preferred handing out library books as an axillary volunteer, right at the start. Tibby, when I read papers by Florence Nightingale, this is not the picture she painted. She talked about education, and helping, and healing. The only healing I ever saw, was in the morgue. The Sisters were okay with me laying out bodies. They said I couldn't do any damage there because they were already dead. That became my job." She cringed at the intimate things required of preparing a body...the routine of packing body orifices and wrapping a body in a shroud. Yet even that hurried task was pressured by time, and the respect for the dead was another idea that never translated into Anna's experience. "All my life you've told me about selfless sacrifice. Oh Tibby, I mean no disrespect, but I need to know it's not a lie! I've thought about how you spoke about dying to self to find life. But... oh! I died to self, and all that seemed to happen was that I just stayed *dead*." Her hazel eyes shone desperately in the firelight.

Tiberius looked at her. Her hair, washed clean and loose, had once shone in a blonde cascade, but now it fell limply over her shoulder. "Anna, these are abnormal times. Perhaps your experience was a twisted, deformed reflection of what our world has gone through."

"But I don't understand Tibby. You've lived a life a service so grandly. I have never once heard you or Marlie complain. How can you live your life like that? You seemed happy enough being bullied by my mother, and even now Grandfield has its own version of hospital hierarchy. I couldn't stand up under it. I felt like a child being bullied at my lemonade stand. It was horrible!"

"Oh Anna... there are wrongs that are designated as war-crimes. And then there are crimes that are never recognised. That doesn't make them no less criminal. What they did was not right."

"Oh Tibby... it feels wrong to mention it because others suffered so much more. I mean... I never even saw active duty. I brought it on myself. If only I was better... quicker... smarter..."

"Oh no, it is not your fault Miss Anna. Malice is never justified. We should not sanitise cruelty just because it happened in a place that is designated for healing. You went to serve your country and was treated as a prisoner-of-war in your own land."

"So how do you do it? How do you serve with such generosity in the face of meanness?"

"For us, coming to Grandfield was a provision. Oh, believe me, plenty thought we were throwing our lives away... working as house-servants for the Whitaker's, but God showed me a long time ago, we can be his hands and his heart to share his love in any station. Besides, at that time, this was a way for Rick to have opportunities we wouldn't have been able to provide if it hadn't been this way. The Whitakers negotiated his fees with the school bursar as part of the conditions of our employment. That benefit was one of the deciding factors for us to come here, but it was not the only one. Marlie loves cooking, I enjoy management. When the war came, it looked like our time was done. I joined the home-guard, but they still needed someone to oversee the hospital, and they still needed a cook. Service-men started to arrive, and my duties were more important than ever. It is a privilege to serve those who have lost so much. We have had a satisfying life here."

"Satisfying..." She lingered over the word, savouring the concept like the bouquet of delicate, fine white roses.

"Anna – satisfaction is from the state of our soul, not the industry of our hands."

"But Tibby, I tried to get the balance. I was determined to do nursing because I knew there was more to life than the merry-go-round of invitations. But honestly, the thought of another urinal or sputum mug will just send me heaving. I've spent enough time with my head in a bucket as it is."

"Oh Anna, you are right. Finding the balance between work and play, service and sacrifice, home and society is necessary. But there is also an internal balance that is to be aligned. Wartime distorts everything until we get used to things out of balance, but we shouldn't assume this is how things are meant to be. Even in peace time, any choice will end up unsatisfactory if our internal equilibrium is unbalanced." Tiberius closed his eyes quietly whispered a prayer. "Oh Lord Jesus Christ, our Saviour..."

"Now Tibby – you are not going to preach another sermon again, are you?" she said reproachfully.

"No Anna – there is no need. Whatever I insight I might offer cannot add to what you've noticed yourself. The truth doesn't need to be shouted to make it more true." He stood then and put another log on the warm embers that had faded while they talked. He picked up another rug Marlie had folded on a chair and wrapped it gently around her shoulders. "Anna, you know that I love you dearly. I believe our life was never meant to be all fight... it was designed to need cycles of rest as well. Wholeness. Shalom. The paradox God offers is knowing that peace is possible even in a storm... or a war."

He left then, quietly opening the door to hear Marlie's gentle breathing under the covers. But he didn't lie down. He quietly paced, just as he had when Marlie was in labour, or when Chrissy was sick, or every day from when Rick had signed up to fight. This was familiar ground... praying for the safe passage of those that he loved, as they traversed the battle fields of life.

Anna watched Tibby leave the room. Her body was weary, her emotions shredded. She just wanted rest. Rest. She sighed. Would God hear her prayer, or would he stand aloof, like her mother staring down her failure with frowns? Or her father melting into the background because that was easier than disapproval? Or Sister Perry declaring her disgust in front of everyone, while she blushed in shame? Surely, such failure would offend the heights of a glorious God.

She gazed into the flames that slowly licked up over the log. Her thin lips were firm. She was stepping off into an abyss and she was not sure anyone would catch her. It felt like walking the plank.

"Dear God..." How? She stopped and tossed her hands in despair. This is ridiculous! When she was young, God was not far away. He was another friend that she would laugh and play with. Together, like Chrissy. But too much had happened. He hadn't fought for her. That was betrayal. Like Henry, God had turned away and forgotten her. That was heartbreaking. "I worked so hard... and what did it gain me? I wanted to be more than a white muslin tea-girl, but I also want more than scrubbing night-waste pans too! Is there no in-between? Am I always to be judged as self-indulgent! Please God! You know I have nothing left. I don't know how to do this." Her hazel eyes spilt over. All the failure, torment, pain, and loneliness that was still raw, came bubbling out. She felt like the little girl who was being glared at by her mother because she had a run in her stocking; being dismissed by her father as he read his newspapers, because she was too noisy. Would God be any different? Impatient, demanding, never satisfied, perfectionistic, too busy?

And then another memory came. She had fallen over and was worried about a tear in her dress. And Marlie had put a salve on her graze, and wiped her eyes so gently, and kindly given her a cool washer for her flushed face. Then Marlie stitched up the rip in her skirt, while Tibby had put aside the things he had been working on, and invited her to climb into his lap. She had fallen asleep in his arms as he sat in his chair. A whisper from Tibby... an echo of past conversations... *"Our God, he is gracious and merciful, slow to anger, and of great kindness..."* Why was the kindness of God so hard to imagine and a severe, judging impatient God more familiar. But as Anna replaced the staring glares of her mother with the compassionate gaze of Marlie... and her father's austere impatience with the warm lap of Tibby, something shifted. This time it felt wonderful to clamber onto the lap of her Father-God who was not hushing her irritably. Her heart scrambled there – urgently, quickly, without hesitation. "Oh God... I need rest... peace. I need you." Somehow that made sense to her. She didn't need to be reproached, or demand a purpose, or apply a solution. She just needed him. Shalom. Again... like a child with a close friend. Or perhaps it felt like climbing up into the strong arms of the trees in the garden. Safe. Elevated. Peaceful. A blanket of serenity wrapped over her shoulders as she rested her head and slept peacefully in His arms.

* * *

12

Anna woke and lay quietly on the lounge listening to the low voices of Marlie in the estate kitchen, preparing breakfast for the residents, the aroma of porridge and scrambled eggs was a relief from the constant aura of Marlie's stinky ointment. The wood smoke from the stove, and the morning warmth of baking bread gave their rooms a comfortable homely feeling. She marvelled at an undefined feeling inside that was fresh and clean, yes – more balanced. Was this the internal balance Tibby was alluding to? She had defined significance by scraping her nails back to the bone, but now she wondered about Tibby and Marlie. It was not their service that made them significant to her, but their generous, big-hearted love. Big enough to embrace each one, everyone. If service was the key... then her mother should have always be pleased. But that was not the case. Few things ever made her mother smile, outside her stemmed cocktail glasses and the perfect gathering of influential faces.

She dozed with a half-smile on her face, as she heard the house bell ring for breakfast. She could hear the servicemen gather in the dining room and the sharp commands of the supervisors organising staff. She could see Marlie in her mind's eye delivering buffet trays to the main dining room, serving out meals to a line of subdued men, bowed in oversized pyjamas hanging on their weak frames. It didn't seem long before the patients were dismissed to their morning exercises. Even though this place was one of the grandest houses in Sydney, it still had the feel of an army camp. Then she heard Tibby and Marlie settle at their own table for breakfast. There was comfort in the predictability of these routines and Anna quietly pulled up the blanket out of sight of the open door and dozed again. It took her a moment to tune into another conversation at the table. A familiar voice, deep and rich, was talking – quiet and indistinct.

Rick! He was home. Already? Marlie had told her that he was not expected for another month at least. Anna stole a glance. She saw him sitting in Tibby's chair, sipping from his mug, and piling a load of Marlie's mulberry jam onto his toast. His thick brown hair that once fell over his eyes with that disarming boyish charm, was cropped short in military efficiency. He tackled another slice of toast with gusto. Her heart quickened and she shrunk back into the lounge. He didn't look at all like the boy who used to take her and Chrissy skimming for tadpoles in puddles at the bottom of the garden after rain; or the serious young pupil climbing trees to study his books in private.

"How long was she like that then?" he asked. His muted voice resonated with concern. Anna snuggled warmly, responding to the compassion in his voice. Marlie murmured something in reply. "But Ma, she has always been so strong. Aren't you shocked that she succumbed so quickly?"

"I don't know about that son. My heart is not reeling from shock, so much as grief."

"Oh Ma. You are right. I am sorry," he said, drinking his coffee. "I guess I just expected her to make it. She always presented with a certain... well... a certain resilience. I guess that is what is so surprising. My memories as a kid made her seem invincible. I never expected her to..." His voice dropped and continued to murmur, his words undiscernible.

Anna's eyes burned and her ears buzzed. Balance evaporated. Rick's undeniable diagnosis of her weakness fell harshly on her battered emotions. Just another nursing sister accusing her of not trying hard enough and not measuring up. Anger rose inside her! How dare he judge? *Succumbed quickly!* It had been a long, drawn-out process of lingering torture! He had seen his own ghouls no doubt, but he had not walked where she walked, up and down the wards carrying the night lamp, so exhausted that she was barely able to put one foot in front of another. She buried her face in a cushion. Fresh tears. Would she ever smile again? His words became white-noise of judgement after that. She dried her tears on her sleeve with a sniff, took a shuddering a deep breath in and exhaled with a groan. Their conversation stopped and she felt their gaze turn through the open door. She was no longer hidden. She rolled her eyes in panic, swiped her eyes again as she noisily made the appearance of waking. She groggily sat up and stretched. She looked shocked, as their gaze connected with hers over the back of the lounge, suitably embarrassed by her position and attire. She huddled one of Marlie's woollen crocheted rugs around her body and hurried off to Chrissy's bedroom. It was still Chrissy's bedroom after all these years. She closed the door on her shame.

Marlie shook her head as she served out another round of eggs. Rick openly gaped at Anna's dishevelled hair and her figure wrapped in colour as she disappeared through the door. Marlie slapped his hand with the egg flip. "Watch it young man," she said sharply.

He raised his brow. "Oh wow... I was." he whispered under his breath in amazement. "That can't be Anna!

"Richard..." she said, warning.

"Ma – what was I to do? I just can't pretend she wasn't there! Is she working here? Is she okay? She looks terrible." And beautiful. And fragile.

"No not working... nor visiting. She will be okay though. She's had a hard time of it."

"Surely she is not going back – to that place?"

"I don't think so..."

"Well, that's a relief. Barbaric places. I can't believe you thought medicine was a good option for me. Almost as bizarre that you and Dad live in a hospital now."

"She's resting. 'Rehabilitating' might be the better term. Just give her some space."

He delved into his eggs, and then paused, and then looked up at his mother. "Mum, I don't know if you've noticed, but... Anna is not my sister."

"And *what* does that mean exactly, young man?"

"It means just that. She is not my sister. Not blood. It's a fact, that's all. You expect me to treat her like one."

"It is right you treat her that way. You grew up together."

"Yes... but well... now we've grown up. She's grown up." He shook his head, his senses reeling. This was a revelation that shocked him, echoing around in his head like the boom of a canon. Where was the spirited young theatre goer he met the night before he was deployed? Or the feisty young friend of his sister who climbed trees like a monkey. This new fragile Anna was different... and it completely took him by surprise.

Marlie looked at him, a similar revelation dawning on her face. A glow of fear tugged at her mother's heart. "Oh Richard... be careful. I know things are changing, but her parents would still never hear of such a thing."

"They wouldn't hear of her going to a hospital either. But she did. How she stayed there for the whole war is a feat of remarkable endurance. She's determined... and tough... and brave. That's for sure."

"Right now she is not tough; she is exhausted and in pain. So, just let her be. Richard – I mean this. She needs rest, and you can't afford to be distracted just as you are getting back into your work, and all."

"Distracted? Well Ma, that really depends..."

"On what?"

"On her." He picked up the last of his toast and left the egg. "I'll go and help Dad groom the horses, so we are not late. It seems so strange not having Pauly here." He lightly brushed his Mum's forehead with a kiss. "I love you, Mum. And I am sorry about Aunt Phoebe. Truly. I know your relationship was complicated, but you loved her."

"She was my sister first and foremost. I will miss her and her hats. Go and help your father get ready. He'll be mighty pleased you're back. And don't take too long with the horses. We need to leave in an hour and a half."

* * *

Anna knew the time to confront her parents was coming. That's what it would be: confrontation – not a reunion, not visiting. She was feeling stronger, but she avoided the inevitable like she used to avoid having her hair done by Hillman when she was young. When Tibby reported that her parents had left the stablemaster's house to go out on engagements, she stole those moments to walk around the garden. The estate garden was reduced to very basic hedges along the avenue frontage. The rest of the grounds had been turned to useful cultivation to support the hospital kitchen or left to nature. Returned soldiers wandered about, sitting on various benches scattered around the grounds. Some of them took to tending the vegetable gardens or pruning the rose bushes or the ornamental shrubs that had gone feral. Anna skirted around their activities with the skill of a covert operator in camouflage. One of the last untouched pockets of the estate was Chrissy's Corner past the bottom fence. She often found herself making her way down there delighting in the feel of grass dragging around her ankles through the fresh smell of self-sown flowers. The old autumn leaves were faded and damp, mulching into the lawn. The last of the jonquils were fading and their stems were bent, but there was still that lingering fragrance that was almost too sweet. This wild, unmanicured garden felt alive... organic, regenerative, thriving. Such a contrast to the sterile barrenness of the hospital wards. Anna passed a hedgerow, now overgrown and unruly, and she listened to the sparrows who had made their home there. She dallied beside a climbing rose, winding itself up through the branches of a shrub so that it was hard to tell which branches belonged to the rose or the tree. This part of the garden had not been subjected to the amateur pruners of the resident patients, and the bushes and shrubs were left to follow their own wild and untamed nature. Anna marvelled at the miracle of perfect blooms through the woody tumble of thorns. As she touched the faded blush of pink rose petals in full bloom, they fell freely into the palm of her hand. She instinctively rubbed the petals between her fingers and noticed their delicate aroma rise as they were bruised. Oh. All those times when she had boiled petals to make her own rose water, yet she hadn't noticed this idea before. Petals smelt more fragrant under the pressure of crushing. Hmm. Noteworthy.

She sat down on the faded bench seat and lingered in the cool shade of the trees, rolling rose petals in her fingers. She closed her eyes and images of that spring birthday afternoon-tea shared here with Chrissy sprang unhindered to her mind. How could something so many years ago, still be one of her happiest memories? Why couldn't life be like that more often?

"Anna?" His step was cautious, and he held his hat in his hand.

"Oh." Her eyes flew open. She had hoped this corner would stay uncontaminated by intrusions... her secret place... away from the reminders of hospitals and pain and patients. But this time there was no escape. She jumped to her feet quickly; a routine drilled into her - subservient and respectful. The old Grandfield was barely recognised in her now. "Hello Rick."

He stepped forward. "Anna... please... sit. I came talk. How are you feeling?"

But she didn't sit. She lifted her palms awkwardly and noticed the smell of Marlie's ointment on her skin. Rose petals were a relief. It felt appropriate that smell was an external measure of her internal healing. "My hands are recovering well. Your Mother's ointment is remarkable..."

Rick frowned as he noticed the smell. "You're brave to apply that so diligently. It still smells like stink-beetles..."

"Yep. That's accurate. But it is helping... and not having an hourly routine of scrubbing hospital equipment for ten hours a day has helped as well." A thought floated past her mind as she held one last rose petal between her fingers. Surely remedies didn't have to smell like a hospital ward or a toilet. Why not like roses? Why not like Chrissy's spring garden of jonquils and violas?

Rick looked into her face, but she avoided his gaze and stared up into the branches of the trees. She felt the heat starting to rise across the back of her neck. His judgement jabbed her again. The shame of her failure was more painful than the wounds on her hands, broken and raw. When he spoke again, she was stiff and defensive.

"Anna – I..." He paused. Rick could feel her anger, but he needed to talk with her. He had begged his father for this privilege, just so he could have a legitimate reason to speak with her. He had tracked her through the garden hoping to talk with her in private, but this was not how he imagined their meeting would be. "I have something I need to tell you. And it will be hard. I need you to be brave in this matter as well." He signalled again for her to sit, and he sat beside her.

"Brave? What does that mean?"

"I know you have asked us not to disclose your whereabouts to your parents..."

"Yes. And that hasn't changed. Don't you dare tell them!"

"Of course. This is something different... Well..." How could he put this? "Your father is not well. He is housebound and does not leave the Stablemaster's residence."

"Oh." She didn't really know what to do with that information. She wasn't ready to visit with him. Not yet.

"And well... there is something else. I wondered if you had heard from your brother?"

"Max? No... but that is not new. We were told his branch of Signallers Corps was a covert operation. But in his letters, he before his deployment he assured me that the work he was doing was as safe as one could get in the war, supporting the troops in the background... decoding and sending messages. What are you saying?"

"Anna, Max has come home..."

"He's home? Here? Oh, I have to go and see him."

"That is what Mum and Dad were hoping... that you might do that. But Anna, he was injured... quite badly..." He saw the panic in her eyes, and he quickly reassured her. "He is recovered now. And quite strong. But he is not seeing anyone and barely eating. And that is a problem. He doesn't want your parents to know he is here either."

"Why? He was always able to handle them much better than me."

"Anna... he lost his leg."

"Oh. Still, lots of people learn to walk with a prosthesis." She stared at him. "What aren't you telling me?"

Rick cleared his throat and wondered if he should have left this news for his father to tell. "He was burnt, but a lot of the scaring is not visible. But he lost his sight. And..."

"*And?* There is *more?*"

Rick nodded. "These are old injuries. He was nursed here at Grandfield hospital during the war, and when he recovered, he went back to headquarters... to some sort of deciphering work. Anna... he cannot speak. The doctors don't know if it is a form of shell-shock, or if the injuries affected his vocal cords in some way."

* * *

Anna had not walked the corridors of the main house since she had come home. She stared at the bare walls. All the ornamental trappings of home had been stripped. Familiar sombre portraits that she hated as a child would have been comforting now. It was barely recognisable. She knocked at the door and was greeted by silence. She heard a shuffling movement inside and tentatively opened the door. She saw him standing by the window, curtains drawn back as if he was looking out over the courtyard.

"Max!" she cried. "You have come home!"

He turned. Shocked. "Gruffling?" the words formed on his lips, but no sound came.

"Yes, it is me! Oh. I am so glad you are safe. I have worried so since I heard you were back." She saw his frown and laughed. "Now – don't you chuck-off at Tibbs and Rick – they knew I needed to see you. Oh, look at you, you ugly old troll... you do me good to see you!"

He shook his head and smiled, and he reached out for a hug. He stepped back and frowned. Max reached for the slate tablet on the table. He felt the borders of the slate with his hand and scratched down a message. "What is that smell?"

"What... this?" She waved her bandaged hand in front of his nose, and he flinched. "It is Marlie's stinky home-made remedy. And as horrible as it smells it is working really well."

His hand trembled. "Get me some. Might help my scars."

"Sure... we can stink like old billy-goats together." She laughed, and she noticed the hint of a smile on Max's face.

Anna spent a lot of time with her brother. She was the only one he would see. Max became Anna's confidant, sharing with him what her experiences had been like. Perhaps he was a safe confessional because he could not argue back... or tamper with her fragile feelings... or tell.

"I couldn't stand it. In fact, if I never have to set foot in a hospital again, I would be pleased – not that I won't visit you here, of course. But the work, I'd very much prefer a firing squad! That's what they do to defectors right? So that might be appropriate. It is a relief the war is over, and I can admit it now. I hated every minute in that nursing uniform!"

Max sat with his slate pencil and tablet and scratched down a message. *"Why not be a secretary?"*

"I was enlisting for the war effort. So many people I knew were helping... Rick, Pauly, Mr Tunstall and even Hillman... and I wanted to do something that was more than a token contribution."

"Hillman?" His body went stiff, and his lip quivered.

"Yes, even my governess was doing something noble. I wanted to as well, but I was never allocated normal nursing duties. I was kept in the back room scrubbing like a maid. But now the war is over, I am done with it."

"You did what was asked. No soldier does less." His slate pencil wobbled as he wrote.

"If that's all it was, I would be okay with it. But Max – they were malicious. Sister Perry was the worst. As soon as I stepped through the door, she was determined to break me. She insisted I was not getting privileges because I lived on Parkland Avenue. But I never asked for any!"

"Drill instructors. Bullies in uniform."

"She made it personal. I've lost count of the times I was hauled over the coals for not making a bed just right; or sent to Matron because my ward didn't pass Sister's white glove inspection. The only dressings I ever attended to, were on my own hands – they started to break as soon as I got there. And when I'd finally managed to clear them up, I had to wash them with carbolic soap to stop them infecting, and they would break out again. I sometimes wonder if Mother had said something. Of course, I will never know for sure. I just refused to give in to them."

"Your Whitaker metal showing. Didn't give in. Be in my troop anytime."

She hugged him for that affirmation. That was high praise.

* * *

13.

In the weeks that ensured, Anna found that each scratched message on Max's slate board was her inspiration. She was on Max's team. Her need to talk was less, and her desire to see Max emerge from his hermit-cave took over. Their father might be unwell, but he had his wife; Max had no one but her. With stubborn determination Max was insistent that no one would see their Captain reduced to such a frail and dependent state, so Anna tried to find ways to smuggle him outside away from the constant smell of carbolic soap. It was easiest to do this in the evening, while the patients were in the dining room, eating their dinner, and the grounds were quiet with the shadows of falling dusk.

Now that her mother's social life had been reactivated after being blown into oblivion by the war, there was not a day on Mrs Whitaker's calendar that was not full. Even the rising tide of the Spanish Flu, the expectation to wear masks in public, and government health directives not to meet in groups, did nothing to restrain her insistence to organise functions. Even though, technically, Tibby and Marlie were no longer employed by Mr and Mrs Whitaker, Tibby insisted on keeping in touch in case they needed support. Every morning Anna would check with Tibby when her Mother was going out. When she left, Anna walked around the grounds unhindered. Anna would be greeted by the sad, lost gazes of patients who sat in the shadows of trees or quietly tended long neglected gardens, and sometimes in the manner of an Auxiliary library volunteer she would encourage them. But unless Max was reassured it was after dark, he refused to go out.

Every Friday and Saturday evening, the gramophone played loudly in the Glasshouse. That became the ideal distraction. While the music blared, and the frantic steps of the Foxtrot and Charleston were tapping away the pain of the past decade, Anna would guide Max away through the dark so they could sit together in the garden under the moonlight. "You know Max, all those times I demanded that you skip out on Mother's parties so I could have you to myself, you never took any notice. And yet I was right. It was a great idea."

Max wasn't quite as enthusiastic. He remained restless, and the quietness of the garden seemed alternately soothe and agitate him. Sometimes they would just get seated on a bench when he would demand that she take him back inside. Yet Anna pushed on. She needed her brother back... the one who used to read her the Three Billy Goat's Gruff, making up the best Troll voice in the world, just to distract her from missing out. Now he was missing out, and she needed to find the thing that would distract him.

* * *

Anna helped Marlie in the kitchen every day. She came in around ten to bake biscuits for afternoon teas that also doubled for supper snacks. The elaborate canapes for evening cocktail parties were a thing of the past; now it was just about bulk and simple. She donned heavy gloves to help prepare lunches and stir stews. Marlie smiled as Anna boxed up another batch of biscuits. "What would your mother say if she knew you were baking plain old ANZAC biscuits for her fancy dos?"

"Oh Marlie, please don't tell. Not yet. I enjoy the distraction of being here. And it doesn't involve wiping up any sort of body fluid. And you don't demand I do the washing up. Cooking is a relief." She reached over and gave

Marlie a hug. "Thank you for allowing me to stay. I think you have saved my life."

"Hush child. You know you always have a place in our hearts and by our hearth. You are with me. I wanted to tell your parents from the start. But Tibby has been very definite we wait until you are ready. I know that I can't make you ready, just because I am. Just know that when you are, we will be here to support you. I think what bothered me most, is that, if it was me... as a mother, I would want to know my little girl was okay."

"I know... I know... but I just need to figure out a plan before I talk to her. Not having my life planned and scheduled is a sin akin to committing murder. It must be so much worse for Max. But once I've figured it out, I will get on that. I promise."

Marlie went over to the bench and looked curiously into the crockpot sitting on the trivet. "What wonderous creation do we have here?" She lifted the lid and stared amazed at a stew of flower petals, leaves and rose-hips. "You are making rosewater?"

Anna swallowed and blushed. "I've put geraniums in there as well. This is another distraction. I used up my own rose water very quickly, so when I got off my shifts, I would go through the hospital gardens and harvest any old blooms I could find. The hospital gardens were so neglected I could trim them without anyone noticing. The geraniums were hardy and survived when other plants didn't. I used the petals and leaves to make up my own combinations. I needed something to cover that famous hospital smell. I was working on these batches for you." She paused and plunged ahead. "I wanted to see if I could use some of the oil extract to cover the smell of your salve on my hands. No offence intended Marlie. Your ointment might work well... but..."

Marlie laughed. "Cologne de la Stink. My grandmother didn't like me calling it that, but it reeks."

Anna sighed with relief. "I'm sure there is a way for it to be healing *and* pleasant."

"Have you found anything that works?"

Anna pulled out some small plain jam jars. She opened the lids and presented the contents to rub on the back Marlie's hand. "I wanted to find something strong enough to cover it. I've tried a few different things... rose, geranium, lavender, jasmine... even citrus... but the amount of oil needed means the salve loses its consistency."

"I like the lavender, I think..." Marlie offered as she inhaled the sample. "But it still has those underlying 'stinky' notes."

"I know. I've also tried gum leaves. The eucalyptus oil is promising. I've asked Rick to find me a book on plant oils from the library... if they have one. But I don't hold too much hope that this particular subject is well published."

"Perhaps Tibby could take you down to talk to the druggist. Errol knows about distilling oils, and if anyone can work out how to retain the composition of the salve, it would be him."

"Really? You don't think this is silly?"

"Silly? No! I think it's a wonderful! You know what we ladies like. A lotion will never be used if it smells like a cattle-yard. But if it smelt like a perfume... oh, I am very confident that would be very sought after."

Anna felt encouraged. "I saw the jar in Chrissy's room that I gave her for her birthday. I always keep the matching jar with me. It prompted the idea that dispensing the salve into elegant glassware might be very appealing. No one would be embarrassed to have this on their dressing table."

Marlie smiled indulgently. "Oh Anna. It is good to see you creating wonderful things again. This reminds me of those summer stalls that you and Chrissy used to hold down by the street. What an enterprise you had."

"I remember Reverend Peters was very concerned I was abusing the Sabbath. But I never sold anything on the Lord's Day. Chrissy was very strict about that rule."

"Tibby is so much more his old self again. He loves all the boys who are here, but you and Max... you are family Anna."

She smiled and shook her head. "I think you are generous to say such a thing. So, let me cook barrels of stew, pots of rice pudding and trays of oatmeal biscuits. I will amuse myself with rosewater recipes... plant oils, and hand lotions. I feel more at home this side of the kitchen, than I ever did in the Grandfield drawing room."

"Well, I am grateful I see your smile again." Marlie said with a laugh. And then she paused. "Rick is coming home this weekend," she commented in an off-hand sort of way. Marlie soberly noticed that Anna frowned and turned away.

"Then I think we should try some mulberry pie. The berries are plump and juicy, and I can enlist some of the patients to pick them. That would be a treat for them. It is not right that the rosellas and magpies are feasting on our harvest, when it is such a favourite," said Anna forcing her voice to sound light.

"Then tonight we feast," said Marlie. "Mulberry pie and thin custard cream." But as she turned away, she prayed, *'Oh God, protect her heart...'*

* * *

14

Anna had found a moment to escape by herself, sitting down in "Chrissy's Corner". Rick arrived home, and he walked through the grounds on the chance he would find her there.

"I wondered what your plans might be," he said as they stood beside each other examining a climbing rose. It wasn't what he wondered at all. "You know... after this... what is the next for Anna Whitaker?"

"Huh. I guess what you actually mean is: am I going back to nursing?"

He shrugged noncommittally.

"Well Richard, I can assure you, I am not going back. Are you pleased?" She turned and left him standing there gaping like a Venus flytrap. It took him a moment to realise she was walking away.

"Anna! Wait!" He ran after her. "Anna...?"

"What?"

"Where did that come from?"

"I have no idea what you mean," she said coolly.

"You expected me to be delighted that you've been rung through a mangle. Our world is destroyed and the people we love have been so hurt. Why would you think that pleases me?"

"Well, you have told me ever since I can remember, that you didn't think I could be a nurse. So, it seems you were right. I couldn't. I trust it gives you great deal of satisfaction knowing you can finally say, 'I told you so'," she said. "Rick Barnes is always right. I didn't make the grade."

"If I'd been right – you wouldn't have lasted a week! Anna, honestly... it tears my heart you went through that."

"Huh. Sure."

He frowned and shook his head. "You doubt that I only want your success and happiness? Why would you think that?"

"Oh please. You have always mocked my ambition to do something different from Grandfield. Lots of things have changed. But this is definitely the same."

"What are you talking about?"

"I heard you talking with Marlie that morning you came home after discharge. You didn't sound terribly invested in my happiness then." If only he knew that he was the last person she ever wanted to disappoint. "I am sorry I do not meet your high and lofty expectations." He fitted the Grandfield shape more comfortably than she did herself. How ironic was that! The Help measured up, but the only daughter of a Whitaker did not.

He stared at her confused. All he could remember from that morning, over eggs and toast, was seeing her emerging from the lounge, stretching her wings like a fragile, beautiful butterfly. She had been wrapped in his mother's colourful crocheted rug. Her hair was falling everywhere like gossamer... looking like some ethereal wood-nymph darting back to Chrissy's bedroom. Oh, how he wished he could wind back the clock and have that eleven-year-old girl again, boldly climbing trees, sitting annoyingly close, trusting in his good-will while he was trying to study. "That morning? Oh. Believe me... I remember..." Something in that moment had lifted the awful horror of the last five years and made it worth enduring. "You took me by surprise. Mum didn't even tell me you were home."

"It is obvious you didn't know. I would expect you to restrain your harsh opinions, if per chance you thought I was in ear-shot."

"Anna? Why would I be talking about you if I didn't even know you were home. We haven't seen each other for years."

She glared at him before she turned to go. "This is so ironic Rick. You survived the war with flying colours, but it has spoiled me, and it has destroyed Max! I doubt anything will ever be the same." There are some things there is no coming back from. Some things stay spoiled... like overripe pears in a fruit bowl. You can't undo that."

"Anna – it wasn't a test to pass or fail. What we've gone through has changed us all. That is a given." He walked with her through the wild grounds back towards the house. "Is that really what you remember from our friendship growing up? All those times we sat in these trees, is that all you heard? That I thought you were spoilt?"

"It is to be expected. I am a pampered Whitaker from Grandfield Park after all."

"Anna, I am so sorry!"

"Sorry I am a Whitaker? Sorry I grew up with privilege? Sorry I am flawed? Sorry I couldn't make it outside the protection of these gates? Do you have no more improvements to suggest on my manners or morals? Sometimes I think you were more my parent than my own mother and father."

He studied her face. There were some things... a lot of things... he had been thinking about. "Anna, you were my kid sister. You and Chrissy were inseparable. I never got one without the other... until... well, until she wasn't there anymore. I missed Chrissy, desperately. I still do. But after... huh, I think... I think I adopted you. I think I wanted you to be my sister in her place... and then I hoped it wouldn't hurt so much. But that was not fair to use you as the instrument to soothe my pain. I'm sorry Anna. I am sorry I made you the project of my grieving... that wasn't right. That is what I'm sorry about. But I was never sorry about you."

She swallowed and her voice softened. "I miss her every day. Is that even allowed? She wasn't my sister. She wasn't my family."

"Why are you talking about? She absolutely was your family! It is right that we miss her. Chrissy hasn't disappeared from our hearts, just because she doesn't sit at our table anymore."

Anna swiped her eyes and swallowed, shaking her head. "I appreciate your candour. This time it is comforting. Your family has always included me. Thank you. Perhaps... perhaps the war has not changed everything."

"Hmm. No one sees what we saw and comes through unchanged. I'm grateful they retained my internship at the firm. Some people came back to nothing. And although an accountant's office is busy, it is a haven when compared to a front-line battlefield. The rules and routines seem reassuring in a way. Safe. Predictable. I think that is why it is not hard for me to be there."

She looked at him and frowned. "Accounting? I thought you were going into business management."

"Hmm. My lecturers encouraged me to apply for accounting. They said it was a baseline skill that was necessary for management. But perhaps they thought I didn't have management in me. Anyway, I transferred over, even before I enlisted."

"But I don't understand. You never deviated from your goals." She frowned. An accountant? It didn't sound like him at all. "Did they think management was outside your wheelhouse because you come from house-staff? Your father single-handedly managed Grandfield for years."

"Perhaps it was the better choice." He shrugged. Indifferent. "Perhaps not. Or perhaps, what I do is less important than who I am," he said as he opened the door and walked inside.

* * *

Max looked up expectantly as he heard Anna's step by the door. He quickly scrawled on his tablet. "Good. You are here. I need you to find Mim."

"Well good morning to you too. Who is Mim?"

"Mim Hillman – your governess."

"Hillman? My governess? Really?"

"Yes. I need you to find her."

"Well, I haven't really heard what she is doing now. But I can ask her father – he still does the gardening."

"Yes – do that."

"Ahh, as in now? Right now?"

He nodded and brushed his hand impatiently for her to get to it. Then he frowned, stomped his cane and held up his hand for her to stop. "No. Don't," he wrote quickly. "I need a suit for the Christmas Gala." He stood up and stretched himself taller.

"Okay... what has got into you? Are you alright?"

"Help me practice for the dance. You can come to the Gala with me."

"I'm not going to any dance, Gala or otherwise. Mother will be there."

"Then we will practice here."

"If you must."

"Yes. That's better. Must get started: Gala is soon." He grabbed his crutch and stood up expectantly.

Anna looked at him curiously. Was Max back? "Oh. Of course... only a few weeks away." Although she was thrilled this idea brought some

128

energy to Max's life, she was less enthusiastic about the dance. The Christmas Gala always brought up memories of Chrissy.

Max felt around for his slate and wrote again. "Better yet, a walk in the garden. Take me to Mim's father."

Anna laughed at that. "Now? My nocturnal Troll wants to go for a stroll in the daylight? What's got into you? Well, for sure. I help Marlie at ten, for the lunch prep. We have time." She helped strap his prosthesis and waited as he tested his weight. "Or... we could just take the chair."

He shook his head vigorously. She guided him towards the door, and Anna felt a weight lift from her shoulders. If Hillman was part of this change in Max... so be it. Hillman had been a good sort really. She might have liked her much better if she hadn't been eleven years old and determined to believe that the whole world was out to oppress her.

* * *

When Rick was home, he would walk with Anna around the garden. She started to look forward to catching up, rather than trying to duck around the hedges to avoid him. She was staring up into the branches of some of the trees in the garden when she heard his voice beside her. "Anna, I was thinking about what you said... about how our experiences have changed us. I know another thing that has changed." He leant against the ribbed bark of the spreading tree and ran his hand through his hair. He needed to say this. "Anna, I said I always thought of you as my kid sister... that has changed."

Anna looked away. Huh. So, he did want to remove her from his family after all? Is that what this was about? More rejection. More failure. Would it ever be okay to just be her... this odd mix of Grandfield and servant? She blinked and refused to let the tears that were stinging her eyes, actually fall. "Each time we have been here, talking in the garden, it has felt more like old times. Not everything has to change, surely!" She swallowed hard.

He looked at her profile, the sun shining through the leaves, and he felt his heart twist again. "You should know Anna ... you are not my sister. I don't think of you like that. Not anymore."

"But it doesn't feel that much different. Can't it stay the same? If I'm truly honest, I really don't want this part of our life to change! Too much change is destabilising."

Rick shook his head. No, in this she was wrong. This absolutely had to change. Actually, it already had. "That morning... when you woke from sleeping on the lounge looking like an angel... your hair falling around your shoulders like a halo. That morning, I realised this had changed for me. Really changed. It hit me like an avalanche."

"Richard!" She was shocked and smoothed her hair down. It felt a little wind-blown. She looked curiously at his expression. He returned her gaze, and she realised this was not how he used to look at her. This time his gaze was sober, soft, affectionate. She felt herself floundering. No... not after what he had said. Eventually there would be moralising and judgement... and she was not up for that. "Don't give me that! I heard what you said."

"What are you talking about? I've already told you I didn't even know you were home."

"You were sitting at the table with Marlie, very intent on giving her an inventory of my failures. That sounded pretty much like the same old Rick who grew up with two kid-sisters."

"Anna. I'm sorry. Please forgive me. Whatever I said... it was wrong."

"But I cannot un-hear what you said! '*She used to be so resilient, but in the end, of course, she would fail so quickly*,'" she said, mimicking the words burnt into her soul. "You cannot deny it."

"What? Why would you think..." His frown deepened as he stood there looking at her. "Is this why you have been so cold and distant? It is not because you needed space to recover, but because you suppose I believe your destiny is some sort of preordained failure. That's absurd!"

"Rick Barnes, I don't even know why any of this surprises me. It shouldn't... not really. Same hat... different colour."

He shook his head, devastated she could not hear his heart. And then he paused, and his frown started to melt as if in some way he was relieved, until his eyes gently laughed at her.

"What?"

"Well, I'm not sure you will not leap to more judgements."

"I think that is the pot calling the kettle black, Rick Barnes. I have lived with *your* judgements all my life."

"Anna – me and Mum... we were talking about Aunt Phoebe. Aunt Phoebe got the Spanish flu, and she didn't make it. She passed after only a couple of days. It was such a shock. *She used to be so resilient, but in the end, she failed so quickly.* Mum probably didn't tell me you were home because I had just got home, and the funeral was that morning."

Anna shook her head dazed. "Aunt Phoebe... with the hats. Her *health* failed? Oh Rick. I'm so sorry."

He nodded. "Yes... our famous Aunt Phoebe... the Milner. A hat for every occasion. You really didn't know?" He paused and coughed soberly. "I am heartbroken over Aunt Phoebe, by the way. She was Mum's sister...

eccentric as all get out, but always robust, in her health and in her manner. It was a shock; it hit Mum hard."

"Oh. I'm sorry... Aunt Phoebe." Anna turned and plucked some gum leaves, rubbing them between her palms, the eucalyptus oil on her fingers smelling tangy and fresh. "I wish Marlie had told me..."

"One thing you may not have noticed, but my Mum is very protective of you. No doubt, she didn't want to add her grief to your worries. Once I knew you were home, she was very definite that I was not to mention any of this to you. She tries to create a bubble of care around those she loves. Sometimes I think she may go too far. I am sure that you are not as fragile as she supposes."

"Maybe... but her kindness has always made this side of the Grandfield driveway a haven for me."

"This is your home, Anna. This is not kindness... it is necessity."

Anna glanced sideways at Rick standing by the trees and noticed a great weight lift from her shoulders. Perhaps he was right. Perhaps things were changing after all.

* * *

They sat in Chrissy's Corner together. It became their retreat place – not just to remember their childhood games, but to sit and talk, away from hospital... and out of range of listening ears. Anna spent a lot of this time thinking about a plan. The plan. The one she would tell her mother about, when she demanded to know what she would do. The way she obsessed over this plan made Anna think she was not so different from her Mother's reputation as an incorrigible planner after all.

Rick fiddled with a twig. "Anna – you are so talented, why did you insist on trying so hard at something that is not you?"

"Ever since I can remember, Tibby and Marlie have told me I am caring and kind. Others would tell me I am a 'people person', with less emphasis on the caring part. By putting those things together, it seemed to me that nursing was the perfect caring people profession. It was supposed to amplify those caring and kind qualities into a serious work. Their faith in me, really had me believing I could do anything. Anything! Even now I don't really understand why nursing wasn't a good fit. The staff were horrible for one. I hardly had any time with the patients because the next task was always there demanding attention. So, the 'people' aspect to nursing, almost seemed incidental... or accidental... or a myth. The Sisters would reprimand me for being tardy if I tried to spend time with the patients. I was abruptly sent off to attend to the next duty. Nothing about it was satisfying."

"You can't blame yourself for the failings of harsh people, even if they disguise it under some sort of system. Sounds no better than Billy Stamford, who was determined to bully you with his fists. You've had a lot stolen from you, Anna, these last years... more than pocket change from a mulberry street-stall."

"Or perhaps it just confirms that I am not a people-person after all." Anna picked some flowers and wound them together in a daisy-chain and put it over her wrist as a bracelet.

"Of course you are! I am just surprised that you thought nursing was the only way to express that."

"I still don't understand why it didn't work. Apart from the obvious reality that I was terrible at it, and I hated every moment. It should have been my way to do something serious."

He shrugged. "Some people have green thumbs; some people build with their hands. Some people prefer numbers; others do words. Some

people like sitting with books; others like working outdoors. Take Pauly…
even with all his oddities, he had found his shape. I don't think life would
have been as meaningful for him, if he never had the opportunity to groom
horses. He loved doing that… even in the army. The Light Brigade was just
another way of doing what was natural for him."

"I never thought I would miss Mr and Mrs Tunstall. I still think that
Mother and Father are living in *their* house. I know for sure I would not like
to have been the one to tell Pauly that his horses were becoming obsolete,
displaced by motorcars."

"The army worked for him. Horses and rules. Pauly pulled his
weight, over and above. Mr and Mrs Tunstall have every right to be proud of
him."

"So Pauly… with all his quirks… found his place, his purpose… and
sacrificed his life to that cause. And me? I am still floundering like an eleven-
year-old without a clue."

"Anna, you never floundered as an eleven-year-old. I just didn't see
you as a person with a healing side. I mean… every sick thing you have ever
touched has died."

"Rick, I don't need this." She considered the flowers on her wrist and
twisted in more violas into the chain.

He leant in and grinned. "But it is true, isn't it? Remember that
sparrow with the broken wing? It was pretty okay, until you got hold of it."

She stared at him in horror and pushed him away. "Are you blaming
me for Chrissy?"

"No! Anna… Oh no! Of course not. I didn't mean that!"

"But isn't that exactly what you said?"

"No! That was not your fault. The doctor said her double pneumonia was not treatable. Dad paid for a nurse to help Mum. They did everything they could, and even they were not able to help. That is not on you! It was not your responsibility to nurse Chrissy. I never thought that. We were children!"

"I know that... of course. But...". Anna stared at the flowers on her wrist. Violas were Chrissy's favourite... among many favourites.

He looked at her and frowned. "Anna? Is Chrissy why you were so determined be a nurse? Did you think it might fix some mistake that you have carried, because you felt you failed Chrissy? Did you think nursing would absolve you of this?"

"I talked about being a nurse even before Chrissy was sick. But... I... I don't know... perhaps it fuelled the idea. I hated feeling not being able to do anything. It was so paralysing. There was nothing... *nothing* I could do."

"There was nothing any of us could do. I felt powerless then... and many times since. Perhaps we both carry some misplaced sense of guilt from losing her."

"But I wanted to do something less powerless. Ironically, that is what I have felt for the last three years with increasing intensity."

"You were so worried about Chrissy, yet you still navigated unknown realms with the courage of Christopher Columbus. Remember how you delivered Mum's message to me at school? You hoodwinked every staid, eagle-eyed schoolmaster into believing you were my sister. I still don't know how you pulled that off. You were right though: there is no way Pauly could have done that. It was a bold move, and a comfort for Mum that I was able to get there so quickly. Which brings me to a confession I must make. I accidently told Mum it was you who brought me that letter. I didn't know you never told her. She was amazed." He leant in close to her. "*That* kind determination is your mark, Anna Whitaker."

"Your argument is that my best traits are being able to pull off lying to Pauly and duping your teachers."

"Why are you so blind to your strengths?"

She cleared her throat awkwardly and shuffled away focussing on the flowers in her lap. "It seems you are determined to enlighten me."

"Well okay... creative, determined, flexible, innovative, persuasive. Even those mulberry-picking afternoons were a mission of gritty resolve. You climbed those mulberry trees yourself so that not a single berry would be missed. Mim Hillman was beside herself. To Chrissy, it was a game. For me, it was a binge. You turned it into an entrepreneurial opportunity. That's got to be a gift."

"I was mad you were eating our profits." She sighed. "We were kids, so it hardly counts. And don't forget that on that last stall, we were robbed blind. All I got was a busted lip and a wounded pride."

"You just picked yourself up and kept selling mulberries."

"I think I need something more serious than berries."

"What I remember is how every customer went away from that little booth, absolutely convinced that their loved ones and their evenings would be so much richer because they had bought your mulberries. That is remarkable. You encourage with such ease and make money in the process. Why is that not noteworthy?"

"Rick I am surprised by you. I need something meaningful. You've got a professional job. Oh, it would have been so simple if nursing had been the answer to this dilemma, but I know it is not."

Richard looked at her thoughtfully. "Anna, I have nothing against nurses – they do great work, but you have to wear the hat God designs for you."

"You sound like Aunt Phoebe. *A well-fitting hat, makes all the difference for any occasion.*" She took her chain of flowers and arranged them in her hair. And started on another one.

"Exactly! It is no shame that the nurses' veil didn't fit you that well. I don't believe that God would go to all the trouble of making us one way and then expect us to invest so heavily in something that clashes with that."

"Huh – Tibby said the same thing."

"I envied Pauly who could not wait to get to work every morning to groom his horses and oil the tack."

"I think it was simpler for him."

"Probably his focus made it simple. But I've thought about this. I truly believe when we find the hat God's designed for us, wearing it won't feel uncomfortable. Regardless of what we do... whether it is a stable-hand, or a house servant, or a nurse, or an accountant... wearing our hat becomes our opportunity to make a difference."

"See how you defy your own argument? Nothing I do makes a difference."

"I couldn't disagree more! Anna, you are the difference... you made Chrissy's life rich and gloriously fun... just by loving her. You did that... by being you... not by working so hard at wearing a hat that doesn't fit well! Look at how you help Max. He has got his swagger back. That is remarkable. If we work as God has created us to be... surely that help us feel more fulfilled."

She shook her head. "But that seems selfish. Tibby has always said we should die to self."

"Selfish? A heart is selfish... not a job."

"Or perhaps it feels too easy... lazy. Almost like having fun. A serious life... a worthwhile life... surely it isn't meant to be easy."

"I don't think it is meant to grind us into the ground either, until we can't stand up. Think of all your Sunday school lessons. Joseph – he saved the world by wearing the hat God designed for him... on Potiphar's estate, in prison, in Pharaoh's court. Nehemiah, Queen Esther and Daniel did the same. It wasn't easy... but they flourished in difficult places."

"You sound like you want me to stay buried here in Grandfield."

"Anna – I don't want you to be buried anywhere. I want you to flourish... I want you to wear a hat that is your own unique style."

"Then why are you so determined to squash me down into the shape of the Grandfield mould? I hate it here!"

"You don't look like you hate it." He smiled at her sitting there, smothered in flowers... "You are creating something beautiful."

"You know what I mean. Over there. That part of Grandfield."

"That part of Grandfield doesn't exist anymore. It has been taken over by a hospital board. Max is negotiating to keep it as a private hospital and rehabilitation centre. He is determined to support returned service men, and to work with them, retraining back into civilian life. He has asked Dad to stay on as manager. He has offered me the accountant's position. The life we grew up with no longer exists for any of us. But different can be rewarding too."

"You are going to do this? You would really choose to come back here?"

"Anna... I've asked for time... whether I take the job is dependent on a number of factors."

"Like what?"

"Like *you*. I need to know what you think about this. Staying here with Dad and Mum, and Max and Mr Hillman in the garden. Making this into something different, and worthwhile. Lots of people need help here... and we can be part of that."

"I've told you I won't do nursing. I can't Rick. It isn't me."

"I don't mean nursing. I think the point about hats is not what we do... but discovering what it is the natural purpose God created for us. We can find a way to wear that hat in any place, even Grandfield. In the philosophy of Aunt Phoebe, when we find the hat that fits us well, it will make a difference, it will be comfortable and we take that hat wherever we go, whatever we do."

"Then what is your hat, Mr Barnes? I find it hard to believe it is accounting and ledgers."

"No... that is my job. I would say that the shape of my hat is that I take a corner that is messed up and chaotic... and bring more order to that place. If I make coffee and cake, I take random ingredients and order them so that they taste delicious. In the army, order was mandated every day. When I am bookkeeping... I take random receipts and put them in orderly categories, so our clients know that part of their business is accounted for reliably so that they can get on with their core-business. That is my hat. Someone else, could do the same jobs, but with a different purpose behind it. No two hats are the same because they are custom fits. Aunt Phoebe understood that."

"Huh. I never thought of Aunt Phoebe as being such a profound minister of purpose."

"Oh Anna, you are remarkable. It is not a sensible job that is your calling, it is finding the right hat for you to wear. Then regardless of what job we find ourselves doing, there is purpose and significance in what we do with all our heart. There is a hat that fits you and has your calling written on the inside of the band. That is your mission for now. Finding your hat."

* * *

Anna pushed some fresh biscuits she had made towards him. And sat down and poured a cup of tea. "Rick, I think I know what is in my hatbox."

"Oh...?"

"I think it is *Resourcing*. I was happier resourcing a sick room with reading books, than cleaning it... but then... if I had been able to think of clean beds and pans as a resource to support the patients, I might have found some sort of purpose in it. The skin on my hands may have still objected but I think my heart may have tolerated it more."

"Yeah, I can see that." He took a drink and considered the biscuit in his hand. "So, in baking these incredible biscuits, are you resourcing me with a great afternoon tea? Does your plan involve opening a teahouse to resource people to connect? You might need some orderly bookkeeping in the background." He liked how this complimented his own hat. They had talked about this idea a long time ago.

"I cooked these biscuits because I know you like Marlie's jam-drops, that's all. Well okay... I am resourcing your appetite... and your willingness to sit with me."

"I am happy to be resourced by you any time."

"As I was thinking about Aunt Phoebe's hats, I was wondering how this hat could transfer into all manner of jobs. You got me thinking about selling berries on the sidewalk. I was resourcing each of my customers even though they all took the berries for a different reason: celebrating a win; comfort in the face of a loss; showing appreciation; health benefits; a special treat; or just a pleasant evening at home. I wasn't so much selling berries for pocket change – I was resourcing! Yes, '*Resourcing*' is my hat." She sat back satisfied, and bit into her biscuit.

Rick's face spread wide in a smile. "I love it." What he really loved was the light turning back on in her eyes. They had been dulled too long. "Do you have specific plans on where you might wear this hat? But not in a tea-room. Am I right?"

"No, not in a tea-room. But... it does involve a recipe. I've been talking with Marlie about her stinky balm – my skin has healed completely! It is true, I don't have my hands in water all the time now, but this is the best they have been. I spoke to Errol, the pharmacist and showed him my samples. He was impressed when he saw the difference between my hands. Even Max finds it soothing on his scars. However, even though the lotion works, it is not marketable. The smell is too disgusting. So, I wondered... what if I could get the same results but with a lovely fragrance. Marlie has given me permission to use the recipe. Errol analysed the recipe for its active ingredients, but the problem is keeping the right consistency. He's swapped out some parts and he is certain we can develop this further. Errol can distil the essential oils, and he is keen to go into a partnership. He has suggested a range of fragrances for people to choose from. He liked my idea of dispensing it into elegant glassware. He also suggested that we offer plain tubs as well, so people can refill their crystal jars. Or it could be the budget option if they could not afford the nice jar."

"Anna, this is impressive!"

"I really want to present it differently to the gawdy tins of goanna oil that hawkers hock from their street carts. They look more like boot polish than balms. Mrs Grimes took some samples to the markets. There is interest in the concept, and some would consider stocking it once we start manufacturing. Even Max said that if I supply a base-line quantity for the hospital, he will stock it in the dispensary. All these people believe in my idea! And manufacturing? That sounds so serious."

"It is serious..."

"Rick... I wanted to ask if you would help me with the business side... and I am going to talk with Father about a start-up loan. I will be wearing my hat... *Resourcing...* my style, my shape, my fit. I am going to call it *Chrystal's Balm...* a play on the idea of the glassware. Marlie liked that. But mostly, it feels like Chrissy is again helping me at one of our summer stalls. We were an unbeatable team."

* * *

15.

After fixing all the food for the Christmas Gala they escaped down into the garden. The music faded as they left the lights of the glasshouse behind. Motorcars and buggies were parking in the driveway, and they could hear the chatter of patients and partygoers laughing above the dance music. "I feel like a kid again, running out to climb the tree where you were reading. I was so adept at hiding my attachment to your family. My affection for you was always my best secret," whispered Anna as they made their way through the garden, keeping to the shadows. "It was too precious to subject it to the scrutiny of my mother."

"Ahh. See you *have* been attached to me for a long time."

"Not just you. Your entire family."

"Anna, I need to tell you: I have accepted Max's offer. I will be staying here at Grandfield."

"Oh. Rick, we have been getting on so well. You know this will change our friendship..."

"Anna – I hope so. I was serious about not thinking of you as my sister. I doubt the friend-zone will work for me either."

She tilted her chin and considered him in the dim light. "Rick Barnes – what are you saying?"

"Anna, I am in serious danger of falling in love with you... not my sister... not my friend."

"But you said you are going to stay. Grandfield does not mix business with personal. And it certainly does not across driveways." She was not scandalised but stood there savouring in the warmth of his smile as the night fragrances of the rose garden infused the air around her.

He searched her face in the shadows of the night. "You said yourself; you have cross that line your entire life."

"How could this even..."

He cut her off. "Okay! I have to tell you. Anna, there is no *danger* of that happening. It already has. I love you sincerely. I can't remember a time when I haven't. But, as I told you before, the 'little sister' fondness... it was once a way to stay close to you, but not anymore. Do you seriously not understand what I am saying?"

She looked away, the frown on her brow creasing. "Hmm. I think I do."

"And? Is this something... you and me... you would consider? You are right... we are from different sides of the Grandfield driveway. Once that would never have had the possibility of growing into anything. But the world is a changed place." His heart stopped as she shook her head soberly. "Oh Anna, no... please don't. Don't tell me that. I don't want to go back to Max and tell him I have to leave... because without you, I can't stay here. I won't."

"It's not that I don't want this, but you know my parents will still resist this. They do not accept that the world is a different now. They want to believe things will go back to the way they were."

"I'm not worried about your parents, or mine. I am asking you. Will *you* resist this? Me? Us?"

"Does this look like I'm resisting? On the evening of the Christmas Gala, I am walking around the night garden with you, rather than preening myself for a dance. For months now, I couldn't wait for Tibby to tell me when my father brought out the motorcar, and I'd get excited when I hear it chug out the driveway, because it meant I could walk around the grounds, and I was elated by the chance that I might meet you there. I help Marlie cook up a feast and then rush through it so we can go for a stroll in the garden after dinner. I like to think that you are falling for me. Finally."

His fear receded as he smiled. "Falling? I think I am past free-fall. I have crashed. Anna, I am crazy about you. Completely."

"I also have a confession of the heart."

"You do?"

She paused. "Well... I was never going to tell you this, but Chrissy and I used to play a game where all the Grandfield servants were the devoted citizens of our very own kingdom. We were very generous sovereigns. Everyone had their role. Pauly was the Keeper of the Royal Stables. Chrissy was the governor, implementing reforms to make Grandfield a more equitable and fairer kingdom for all. And I... I have wanted to be your princess ever since gallant Richard the Brave, son of King Tiberius and Queen Marlie, rescued me from The Terrible Tower, otherwise known as the camphor-laurel tree behind the stables."

He laughed. "Anna? How old were you when I pulled you out of that tree? Six or seven? All this time I had your heart? Oh, your silence is cruel."

"Chrissy was quite resolved that I would grow up to marry Prince Richard, so she could be the bridesmaid... and we would be sisters legitimately. We planned your wedding quite often."

"You both plotted my romantic demise?" He bowed gallantly with a smirk. "Your liege, my Lady... I humbly submit to your collective wisdom. It would not be fair of me to resist such determination, even though it seems my role is quite incidental to your sisterhood pact."

"It was a game... but I completely believed it. I had such a crush on you. I still do."

"I remember you insisting that I coach you in tree-climbing. I don't think there is a tree in this garden we haven't climbed a thousand times since. Perhaps you really are a wood nymph... with magical powers to render me powerless under your spell."

"So... if you are a prince, masquerading as an accountant... and I am a woodland faerie princess disguised as an abandoned nurse, as romantic as it is, it doesn't sound like a hopeful match. And that scares me. Real life is not a childhood game... and yet part of me still wants to go back to those glorious, fearless, blissful days."

"Anna, you should know Mum shares your concern. She fears Grandfield's traditions still hold the balance of power. Are you up for that?"

Anna frowned. "You can't mean Marlie and Tibby? I don't believe you! Even today... Marlie was saying how..."

"Of course, they both love you dearly. But she is terrified what will happen now I want to marry you!" It was out before he realised. He stammered at his outburst. "Sorry... I didn't mean to blurt it out like that."

"Really? You do want to *marry* me?"

"Oh Anna." He looked into her eyes. "That was seriously lacking finesse. I had hoped my declaration would be more in keeping with your sense of a royal romance, but it is true none the less..."

"Why is this such a shameful thing to confess?" She looked confused.

"No, not at all! I love you... but the timing, and our diverse situations." He cringed. "Who knows if this thing with Max will work out. Falling out with your brother whom you have idolised forever... how could we ever survive that? Ma warned me that I needed to back off. But I haven't. I'm sorry."

"I'm not sorry. I thought any time would be perfect to share such a sentiment."

He held her hands and turned them over. There were faded scars beside the pink skin that was still tender and soft from healing, and he gently pressed them to his lips. She pulled her hands away, and he frowned, disappointed. A deep sigh escaped. Then she took his face between her palms and kissed him gently. He responded with relief, holding her tight. Fiercely. "Oh Anna." He backed away and looked at her tenderly. "Are you sure?"

"Completely." And they sealed their confidence with another kiss. "I finally have my prince."

He pressed her hand over his chest. "I do not want to rush you, so we will keep this private, until you are ready to disclose us... and then we will manage their reactions together... however they take it."

Together. Marlie had said the same thing. *Together.* No one was telling her she didn't belong. Anna felt infused with more strength... like the healing balm on her hands was working on her heart. She knew two things now: the fear was gone, and the formation of her plan was materialising into tangible steps. She smiled and paused, looking up at him with her head tilted. Eventually she took a breath. "So, was that long enough to hold this in your heart, because I am ready to share this most fantastic news to the world. Right now."

"Straight away? Even with your parents? Really?"

"I have waited so long for this, it is far too grand to keep to myself for a moment longer."

"Well then... let's see how they take it. This should be good." Rick made a sweeping bow and offered her his arm. "Stand your ground Anna Whitaker and be the courageous Princess that you are," he said with a gallant bow. "We have a Christmas Gala to attend."

Her heart felt light as she slipped her hand through his elbow, and walked together towards the Glasshouse, lights pushing back the shadows while music was pushing out the silence. Some guests were starting to leave, and a motorcar spluttered along the sweeping driveway and backfired as it went through the front gates with a lurch. Her Mother's fabulous Christmas Gala would continue well into the night, an annual exemption of the usual ten o'clock curfew. And then there was the fundraising count to be attended to. As the newly appointed accountant of Grandfield, Rick was required to supervise that.

Anna smiled. Yes, it was time. She was not facing the future alone. They both were criss-crossing back and forwards to different sides of Grandfield Park. She was part of the change to take down the divide. On grand occasions, and in small unnoticed moments, Anna had many people to resource, and in that, she had found the shape of what her life could be. It was time to face her destiny... and she adjusted her well-fitting hat with a smile and took Rick's hand ready to dance.

⌘ ⌘ ⌘

The end

Other books by this author

Matt's Boys of Wattle Creek

Maggie & Minotaur

Rose's Diary

Gems of Australia Series:

Sapphires of Hope

Rubies of Ambition

Emerald Dreams

Homes of Healing Series:

The Beachside Cottage

Petrea Downs

The Writer's Retreat

Guthrie's Lot Series:

A Spacious Place

A Level Path

The Crying Tree

Pioneers of Grace Series:

Time of Grace

Circle of Grace

Journey of Grace

Mask of Grace

Crucible of Grace

Sculpture of Grace

Bottlebrush Grove Series
Shadows in the Corners
The Ragged Edges
Scratches across the Surface
Cracks through the Core

Children's Book
The Bush Olympics.
The Great Fly Hunter

Non-Fiction
Reflections in the Bible – Daniel
Reflections in the Bible – Abraham
Reflections in the Bible – Elijah
Reflections in the Bible – Job
Reflections in the Bible – David
Reflections in the Bible – Elisha
Reflections in the Bible – Joseph
Reflections in the Bible – Kings of Judah
Reflections in the Bible – Nehemiah
Reflections in the Bible – Samuel

www.ingramcontent.com/pod-product-compliance
Lightning Source LLC
Chambersburg PA
CBHW051705180726
48283CB00004B/1219